To

The

Sugarplum

Ladies

Romans
8:
37

I pray this story
resonates with you!

Carrie Fravatt Kzgh

The Sugarplum Ladies

By

CARRIE FANCETT PAGELS

HEARTS OVERCOMING PRESS

ISBN: 978-1-7366875-5-0

This is a fiction book. Places, names, incidents are either imaginary or they are used fictitiously. Any similarity to actual people, events, or organizations is coincidental.

Hearts Overcoming Press

Printed in the United States of America

DEDICATION

Dedicated to Debbie Lynne Costello,
My Dear Friend—
A wonderful author and critique partner
and a blessing from heaven.

&

In Memory
of My Aunt,
Wilda Jane Roat Fancett
Always an encourager, always a gracious lady,
always loved!

Prologue

Detroit, 1867

*I*t was now or never—Eugenie Mott must either confide in her father and hope for the best or remain silent and bend to his wishes. She yanked the velvet curtains closed to the September sun in the parlor. Eugenie didn't wish to disappoint her beloved father. She rubbed her hands together in agitation as she paced back and forth. The burgundy and gold wool carpet that covered the wide oak planks of the floor was as tightly woven as her gut felt.

Horace Ontevreden had become one of Father's closest companions only recently. How had he influenced her father so greatly in such a short time? The man was over twenty years her senior. The way he'd charmed her father reminded her of some smarmy medicinal oil salesman luring a matron into purchasing his ineffective—or worse—wares. He was, though, after all a merchant so perhaps that was simply his manner.

From the beginning, both Eugenie and her housekeeper, Lorena, had judged Horace to have sprung from the lower classes. Not that she was a snobbish person—not anymore. But if she were to influence Detroit's upper echelon of social circles then Eugenie must have a husband of satisfactory character and possessing good manners. She wasn't sure Mr. Ontevreden was acquainted with either. But what did it matter? He was unlikely to allow Eugenie to engage in anything other than tasks which would support her role as wife of an importer of fine porcelain. He'd told her father he'd intended to keep her at home—where she belonged—instead of out pursuing social missions as she had been doing.

"Miss Mott?" Mary pushed a cart into the parlor. The scent of coffee and apple Danish permeated the close quarters. "'Tis from your own batch of dough that you mixed up last evening."

"Oh." That meant the pastries were likely to be tough.

"You can dip them in the coffee, miss."

"What time does Mr. Ontevreden arrive?"

In the hallway, Father's tall clock chimed the hour.

"Anytime now, miss."

"Is Father still in his library?"

"Yes, miss."

Which meant he was still working on an announcement that he intended to submit to the *Detroit Free Press*. Eugenie's heart clenched in her chest. Mr. Ontevreden had pressured Papa to have the notice placed in the paper even before Eugenie had accepted his proposal. Why on earth had her father agreed?

"Should I pour for you, miss?"

"No." Regret would be the bitterest drink to swallow, if she went through with this. But with Papa feeling so poorly of late, she wanted to bring him comfort. And Mr. Ontevreden was indeed a man capable of taking care of Eugenie.

Too bad Papa couldn't see that Eugenie was capable of taking care of herself. Not only of herself, but of the ladies who attended her meetings at the public auditorium along the river. Ladies who had lost everything. But now, with her inheritance from her mother, Eugenie was free to explore ways of assisting the many Civil War widows and their children. Not that Papa would approve of such a venture. Then again, perhaps he would.

"Mr. Ontevreden isn't such a bad-looking fellow, miss. I'll give him that." But Mr. Ontevreden was much closer to their aging Irish servant's age that he was to Eugenie's. "And he always attends services at your church."

"That's a good thing." Too bad he didn't seem to be listening to the preacher. Instead, Horace would surreptitiously scan the congregation.

"Beggin' your pardon, Miss Mott, but have the two of you actually met with Reverend Hogarth yet?"

"No." Eugenie adjusted a satin bow on her new Worth gown. She had a weakness for pretty clothing but since working with her ladies, most impoverished, she'd taken to dressing in more drab clothing. With guilt, she admitted to the delight this beautiful cream and blue ensemble brought her in wearing it. Too bad her crinoline, a new purchase, dug into her waist.

Mary cast her a sideways glance. "One wouldn't know you were already thirty years of age, miss. Not with that lovely skin of yours and your slender waist."

Had anyone else but her erstwhile parlor servant uttered such words, Eugenie would have been mortified. But she knew Mary intended no harm.

From outside the room, in the hallway, voices carried.

Lord, I know my father wishes me well, but please help me out of this situation.

Amen.

Chapter One

*H*ow strange to have tea set only for one, without Father. His recent sudden death had left her stunned. Strange how familiar routines, such as teatime, offered a semblance of comfort. Eugenie rang her mother's silver Austrian bell. In a few moments, Lorena, their housekeeper, and not Mary, slid the parlor's paneled mahogany pocket doors back.

"Yes'm?" Lorena averted her gaze.

"Is Mary feeling unwell again?" She must be, for Lorena to be answering the bell.

Lorena's dark uniform almost matched Eugenie's black bombazine mourning gown.

"Yes'm. Poor Mary be poorly today. But I'll help."

"Thank you."

"Is the tea set up yet?" Eugenie forced a smile.

"Yes, ma'am." Lorena glanced toward the fire. "Let me stoke the fire, too, while I'm here."

The housekeeper possessed a butter-soft Southern drawl that elicited feelings of warmth and yet also a concern for what she'd been through. Lorena had come to them after the war and had grown up as a slave on a Virginia plantation.

As Lorena tended the fireplace, Eugenie surveyed the sumptuous room. Everything in this house was hers, from the wool rugs beneath her feet, to the silver candelabra, to the leather-bound books in the ornate case on the far wall. She had no one with whom to share these earthly goods, but she hoped that would be changing soon, as she desired to use some of her own furnishings to decorate the lodgings she planned to purchase for her ladies. They worked so hard—most Civil War widows, though not all, and were learning a new way of life. Eugenie, too, would have to overcome and persevere, as she encouraged her trainees to do as they acquired new skills.

Oh Papa, why did you go now? Was it so she wouldn't have to marry Horace? She exhaled a sigh of relief. Was it wicked to be so relieved that she didn't have to marry Horace?

Lorena turned to face her. "You all right, ma'am?"

"Missing Papa." But not Horace.

"We all are, miss." She bowed slightly. "I'll bring your tea right quick."

"Thank you. Some of the trainees are impoverished due to other reasons. We aim to help those who are willing to learn."

As Lorena left, Mr. Morgan, the family's butler, entered. "Attorney Christian Zumbrun has sent the papers for you to sign."

"Thank you."

He handed her the creamy envelope and left. She went to the desk and opened the seal, then unfolded the letter and scanned for the conditions of the rental agreement. Although her mother had left her a monthly stipend, she'd not been able to afford a building rental for her ladies—until now.

From the hallway, the clatter of the doorknocker sounded. Not expecting anyone, she stood and took several steps toward the pocket doors to close them. When Eugenie spied Horace's shiny pate, she ducked back. What was he doing here, unannounced?

In mere moments, Morgan entered the room with Horace right at his heels. Eugenie felt her eyes widen. Horace hadn't sent a calling card nor had he waited to be announced. Instead, he pushed past her butler and opened his arms to her as if to embrace her. Eugenie took two steps back, positioning her mother's desk chair between herself and the man who wished to become her husband.

"Mr. Ontevreden, how surprising to see you."

His already pale face blanched further as he glanced between her and Morgan. "Eugenie…"

She cringed, wishing she'd not allowed him to use her Christian name. "What is it you need, sir?"

He rubbed his short silver beard. "Why, I've come to express my condolences, of course."

At the funeral service, he'd at least had the gentility to sit quietly, albeit in the row behind her, which would have held extended family members had she any who had come to sit there.

"Thank you." She should say something to him. Should at least let him know something. But no proper engagement had ever occurred. This didn't seem the time nor the place.

He ran his tongue slowly over his lower lip, reminding her of a beggar about to snatch up a roll and devour it. "I wondered how I could be of comfort to you during this time."

Had they ever actually courted? Were her father's attempts at putting them together over and over again supposed to count as an official courtship? This "relationship" had been nothing like what she'd experienced with Pascal before he'd been killed at Antietam. Her precious beloved. Tears welled up.

"There, there, my dear." Horace pulled an embroidered handkerchief from his pocket and handed it to her. Was it her imagination, or was that one a woman would normally use? And the initial on it wasn't his.

"Thank you." She pressed the linen square to her nose and inhaled the distinct scent of rose, not a scent a gentleman would wear.

Lorena rolled in the tea cart. Her lips formed an *O,* for the tea was set only for one. "Excuse me, Miss Mott, but will Mr. Ontevreden be staying?"

"No," she blurted out. "I'll be taking tea alone."

"Yes, ma'am."

"No, Miss Mott is wrong." Horace's imperious tone caused Eugenie's spine to stiffen. "I will be staying."

Lorena, apparently cowed by the older man, backed from the room.

Morgan stepped forward. "The newspaper has arrived, Miss Mott."

"Thank you. I'll read it as soon as you can escort Mr. Ontevreden out, as he will *not* be staying."

The butler nodded toward the paper. "Your attorney sent a message that you may wish to take note of the society section."

Horace rocked forward and back, as self-satisfaction etched itself upon his aquiline features. "As your fiancé, I'll be staying so we can discuss our plans."

She glared at him. "You, sir, are not my fiancé." Eugenie grabbed the newspaper and opened it to the society section. At the top of the page, in large type-face font, was announced, "Miss Eugenie Mott to Marry Mr. Horace Ontevreden." The pages slipped from her hands to the floor and Horace scooped them up.

"As you can see, indeed I am your affianced."

Windsor, Ontario

How had Percy landed in such a backwater town? By being engaged in a profession, that was how. Seemed the Gladstone family had too many barristers in England. Percy's many social causes had caused his father no end of embarrassment, and he'd been shuttled off to Canada. Percy opened his office window's heavy blue brocade curtains and peered out. On the street below, carters carried goods to the market, with apples, potatoes, and cabbages piled high. Carriages rolled over the hard-packed earth. Lone riders hitched their horses to the posts by the boardwalk. Hard to believe that only a narrow body of water divided this tiny hamlet from both another country and a Michigan city teeming with people.

A heavy rhythmic rap at the door identified his secretary, who entered.

"Mr. Gladstone?" Antoine stood in the doorway, a stack of legal briefs in hand. "Miss Feuerstein is on your docket before you head off to court."

"Thank you." Why had he accepted the case with this young woman? He'd have to hire a detective to help him and in this small town that wouldn't be easy.

It had started when Percy had been invited to dinner with a fellow barrister, and a single woman was seated beside him.

Miss Feuerstein had confided that she might need legal help. An older businessman from nearby Detroit had been pursuing her, and she was considering accepting the Michigander's proposal.

Antoine remained in the doorway, rocking on his heels. "She's here now, sir."

"Bring her in."

Miss Feuerstein, a handsome brunette, was in her mid-thirties if he guessed correctly. Bedecked in an attractive day suit, fashionable even by London standards, she entered the room and greeted him with a demure smile, eyes downcast.

"Welcome." He gestured toward one of his twin black Windsor chairs. "Please have a seat."

He assisted her into the chair.

"Thank you for meeting with me."

Percy went behind the desk, always preferring to put a little distance between himself and a female client. Antoine left Percy's door open to the hallway, an unspoken understanding they had when a solitary woman was inside. His secretary nodded at him and departed down the long corridor.

Percy sat down, and then centered his notepad on his desk. "How may I help you?"

With hazel eyes and a heart-shaped face, this lovely woman should have been married long ago. Perhaps she had been.

"Mr. Gladstone, I shared with you that I've been offered a proposal of marriage by a gentleman who seems to travel in high circles on the American side of the water. However, I'm finding that my American friends have been unable to learn much about him. So I fear I'm in a quandary."

"I see." Percy rested his elbows on his desk and steepled his fingers in front of him. "I'm afraid I'm not a detective, Miss Feuerstein."

"Can you at least offer me legal advice?"

"That I can do." He dipped his pen in the inkwell.

He listened for nearly an hour, taking copious notes, all the while tallying up the cost of taking this case. Detectives were scarce as hen's teeth in these parts, as his southern cook, Sabina, liked to say. But he'd appreciate the extra income for Christmas gifts to his staff, both at home and at the office. He wanted to be a generous employer, not a tight-fisted Scrooge like in Dickens's long-titled novel, *A Christmas Carol, in Prose, Being a Ghost Story of Christmas*. The author should shorten that title to something a little more catchy.

Miss Feuerstein offered him a tight smile. "I guess that's all there is to it."

"I see."

Movement in the hallway caught Percy's eye. His secretary took the arm of a frail white-haired woman whose shawl-covered narrow shoulders were stooped with age. Antoine led her to a bench and approached Percy's still-open door. As he'd been instructed, his assistant was to interrupt him when precisely one hour had elapsed. But Percy had not yet decided if he'd take the case.

"Miss Feuerstein, would you excuse me for one moment?"

He went to the hallway and closed his office door behind him as Antoine met him. "I don't remember having an actual next client," Percy said in a low voice.

Antoine smiled. "That, sir, is my mother. Or rather, the woman I call my mother."

"I'm sorry, either she is or isn't your mother, which is it?" His clerk was only in his twenties, and this woman looked to be well past seventy years.

"She's my *grandmére*. But she raised me."

"I see."

"She's asked if I might spend the holidays with her in Toronto."

To his chagrin, Percy well knew that his secretary couldn't afford such a journey without a Christmas bonus. "Could we discuss this after court today?"

The younger man glanced down at his well-polished shoes. Antoine kept himself neat, never missed a day's work, and was loyal and trustworthy. He deserved both a rest and reward. Why should Percy put off till tomorrow what he could do today?

Antoine murmured, "*Certainement, monsieur*."

Bending toward him, Percy whispered, "My First Day gift to you shall be the fare to transport you home. And my Twelfth Day present, the funds to return."

His clerk raised his blue eyes to meet Percy's gaze, a grin splitting his narrow face. "Thank you, sir!"

"And there shall be an envelope with funds for you to purchase some trinkets and treats for you and your grandmother on the days in between, eh?"

"Oh, sir!" When Antoine moved forward as if to embrace him, Percy took a step backward.

He raised his hand. "You've well earned it."

"You are too kind. *Merci*."

And in need of more business. Percy returned to his office. "I'd be happy to assist you, Miss Feuerstein."

She rose with the dignity of any lady presented at the queen's court. "Thank you."

He escorted her to the door. When she departed, he closed his door and slumped down in the closest wing-back chair. Time to see his friend, Christian Zumbrun, for help.

The past twenty-four hours passed in a swirl, like the quick Lake Huron tempest that had kicked up and then calmed so that Percy could take the ferry across to Detroit. He hailed a taxi and soon found himself at Christian Zumbrun's law practice and greeted by his old friend.

Inside the gothic-style stone building, his friend's office reflected a life well-lived even though it reeked of the thick cigars of which he was so fond.

Percy pointed to the shuttered windows behind Christian. "Open the blasted windows, man, and let some of that smoke out." He waved away the blue haze.

Christian smiled his lopsided grin and complied, twisting the metal handle and releasing the mullioned window outward. "Will that satisfy you?"

"Wait! That might summon the fire brigade volunteers. And with a city of this size, and enough buckets, your legal briefs might all be ruined when they come rushing to this office swinging water around." Percy laughed.

Swiveling to face him, Christian shook his head. "What a lovely thing it must be to have no vices. How do you do it, Percy?"

"Very funny." He shook his head. "If my mother ever pays me a visit, I'll have her review a list of my shortcomings with you."

"No chance of that happening, though, is there?" Christian coughed.

"My mother venturing to the wilds of Canada and out to the backwater of Windsor?" He gave a curt laugh. "About as much chance as me hosting you and your wild boys for Twelfth Night!"

The Zumbrun boys were probably no more rambunctious than others their age, but put them all together in one room, and *voila!* – a disaster was sure to happen. Would Percy ever be a father? He rubbed at his jawline, which could have used a sharper blade.

"Well, you're not here about that, are you?" Christian poured himself a short snifter of brandy. "Have some?"

"No, thanks. I'm here to get advice about a case. And to ask which private detectives might be available."

"Hmm." He took a sip and replaced the stopper in the crystal brandy flask. "I can think of one or two."

"My client is considering a marriage proposal from an American."

"Someone from Detroit?"

"Yes." Percy eyed Christian's beautifully gilt-framed diploma from Harvard. Percy's own, from Oxford, had been framed by his first client in Windsor—a lumberjack falsely accused of theft. The man paid Percy's legal fees by carving a thick frame with bear, pine trees, deer, pinecones, maple leaves, and so on, indicative of life in Ontario. The woodsman had said, "Because now you're one of us, and I hope this will remind you."

Christian cleared his throat. "What do you know about this man who is offering marriage?"

"He's reported to be a prominent member of Detroit society, but I've not heard of his name." Percy slouched into the nearby padded leather-seated chair. "A Dutch name."

"That could be maybe a quarter of my fellow Michiganders." Christian crinkled his nose. "Including my beautiful wife."

"He's supposedly a wealthy merchant."

His friend touched the side of his nose. "Supposedly is the operative word."

"Yes. My gut tells me this man is a charlatan."

"I've always trusted your gut, Percy."

"Then you'll help me?"

"Let me see what I can do."

Chapter Two

Detroit, Michigan

*C*lutching the newspaper tightly under her arm, Eugenie mounted the steps into the dark-red brick building, careful to keep her skirts tugged aside to avoid tripping. How easy it must be to climb these infernal stairs in a pair of trousers. Alongside her, a dapper young gent attired in a burgundy tone-on-tone striped suit hurried upstairs in a flash. She exhaled a long sigh. At least he'd waited at the top to hold the door for her. Slender, with a mop of golden-brown hair, and possessed of an easy grin, the young man reminded her so much of Pascal that tears sprang to her eyes.

"Thank you for holding the door."

"No trouble at all, ma'am." He nodded then headed off in the opposite direction from her attorney.

Eugenie followed the corridor, eying the narrow wooden benches that lined either side of the hall. On the left, a mother with two young children tried to keep them occupied by reading a storybook. On the opposite side, a silver-haired gentleman leaned on a narrow ebony cane propped between his open knees. The poor thing looked like he might keel over at any moment.

She continued toward Mr. Zumbrun's office and stopped at his assistant's desk in a cubby hole adjacent.

Mr. Logan looked up. "Good morning, Miss Mott. Mr. Zumbrun is expecting you." He rose and came from around the desk stacked high with files.

The door to the attorney's office opened and a tall man with thick, wavy, dark hair stood there, his hand on the doorknob, leaning in. His profile was very striking. Eugenie, hesitated to follow the assistant. Instead she stood and watched. Attired in superfine wool expertly tailored to his athletic frame, this man had a presence. But she wasn't here to gawk at handsome men. She was here to speak with her attorney. The distress over Horace's publication of their false engagement must be addressed. Mr. Zumbrun simply had to sort this out.

His client seemed in no hurry to leave, however. The handsome man's laughter carried into the hall. Eugenie took several steps forward and discerned that he spoke with a British accent. Finally, he turned and grabbed his coat from the rack and laid it over his arm. He looked up at Eugenie and his dark eyes widened. The stranger stood there for a moment, looking perplexed. She didn't recognize him. She'd have remembered. Would have definitely recalled those strong, handsome features.

Mr. Zumbrun tapped on his client's shoulder and finally the man moved out into the hallway as Mr. Logan moved past and announced Eugenie.

She should keep her eyes downcast. She should walk right past the stranger as she entered. She should…

"Good day, miss." This close, as he ambled past her, she could smell his piney scent mixed with cloves and something else—maybe bergamot.

Eugenie couldn't manage so much as a nod. She stared like a ninny before Mr. Logan gently took her arm and led her into the office.

"Excuse me for a moment." Mr. Zumbrun shoved a broad hand through his wavy golden hair and hurried out after the departing Englishman.

"Have a seat, Miss Mott." Mr. Logan gestured to one of a pair of heavy walnut chairs, their seats padded and upholstered in dark, masculine leather.

"Thank you."

In a moment, the attorney returned, followed by his previous client. "If it's all right with you, Miss Mott, I'd like Mr. Percival Gladstone, a barrister from Windsor, to also sit with us. He may have some insight."

How embarrassing it would be to recount her dilemma in front of this handsome stranger. But if he could help, why refuse?

When Eugenie nodded her consent, Mr. Zumbrun closed the paneled door and took his seat behind the desk.

Mr. Gladstone took a seat beside her. A smile tugged at his lips. He truly was the most attractive man she'd ever met.

If Percy had known Christian represented such beautiful clients, he'd have come over to Michigan more frequently. This young woman smelled like delicate meadow wildflowers, which pleased him immensely, reminding him of the fields around his home in England.

"Are you paying attention, Percy?"

No, I'm appreciating the lovely lady's creamy complexion. "Hmm? Yes, what was that?"

"I said, Miss Mott has a situation that we'll be addressing. I believe her faux fiancé and your client's want-to-be fiancé may be one and the same man."

Christian and Miss Mott proceeded to describe her suitor.

She procured a *carte de visite* from her reticule and handed it to him. "This is his card."

Percy chortled. "It's him."

Miss Mott's eyes widened at his outburst and Percy struggled to put his best "barrister's face" back on.

She tipped her head at him, fixing him with her intense gaze. "Why so gleeful?"

No detective fees, for one thing. "Well, Miss Mott, you have solved my case."

"How is that?" Her tight voice held censure.

Christian cleared his throat. "Now Mr. Gladstone can let his client know that Horace was already engaged."

"What? He has proposed to another?" Miss Mott pressed a hand to her face.

Percy nodded gravely. "Indeed, to a young Canadian woman of some means."

"But, but…I am not engaged to this man. It is a farce. I never accepted." Dark eyebrows raised high; she'd be a formidable foe in a courtroom. And likely delightful in parlaying intelligent conversations over the dinner table. He could picture her quirking those eyebrows in challenge at him and him teasing her.

"Good." Why had Percy so quickly said that? His face heated. *Good grief, man, get ahold of yourself.*

Both Christian and Miss Mott stared at him.

"How does that benefit you, if she's not engaged to him?" Christian sat straighter in his chair, his eyebrows drawing together.

Percy swiped his hand across his jawline. "Well, of course it is good she's not engaged to a charlatan who would propose to two *beautiful* young ladies."

"*Two wealthy* young ladies." Christian gave him a cautionary glance.

"That's what I said."

Miss Mott gently tapped his hand with her gloved one. "No, you said beautiful." Her lips quirked as though she might be stifling a laugh.

Time to leave. Miss Mott possessed a lovely and regal appearance—just the type of woman his mother always hoped he'd marry. He rose. "Since you hadn't given your consent, Miss Mott, then Mr. Ontevreden can't force the marriage."

She drew in a deep breath and exhaled it forcefully. "That's a relief."

"I wonder, though, if my client might yet foolishly have him as husband." Percy's gut clenched at the thought.

The dark-haired beauty squared her shoulders as she moved toward the edge of her chair. "As long as I am under no obligation to him, I'll be happy."

Christian offered her a Cheshire cat grin. "No consent, no engagement—despite this announcement in the paper. And I've asked Mr. Logan to check at the newspaper to see who posted the ad."

"I cannot believe Papa would have done so."

"Nor I." Christian frowned.

"If you'll excuse me, I'll take my leave." Percy rose.

"Certainly. Sorry to keep you, Mr. Gladstone." She smiled up at him.

She'd remembered his name. A little thrill of victory coursed through him. "Miss Mott, a pleasure to make your acquaintance." He took her small hand and raised it to his lips. Was it his imagination, or did her fingers tremble?

Chapter Three

Detroit

*P*ercy shouldn't be this excited to attend a lecture. But ever since he'd met Miss Mott, he'd longed to see her again. After the legal conference was over, he'd stop by Christian's place and see if Miss Mott had been by his office again—and had she mentioned him? *Pathetic. Simply pathetic.*

The carriage hit a rut and jostled him. Soon, they stopped in front of Gratiot Hall, an imposing brick building. He paid his fare and headed up the walkway. Gentlemen in their long coats and tall hats strode purposefully up to the wide doors and entered.

Once inside, Percy searched the entire building for his event—an attorney's international convocation. The joint Canadian-American Legal Conference invitation had arrived from Christian two days earlier. Must be some new association, as Percy had never heard of it before. After inquiring at several offices, he was about to give up.

A clerk, arms loaded with files, approached him. "May I help?"

"I was told my conference was here at Gratiot Hall."

The man's thin moustache quivered. "The main hall is downstairs and the conference is well underway."

"Thank you." But Percy had seen no sign indicating a legal conference there.

He hurried back down the stairs. He headed toward the massive entryway to the auditorium.

The scent of Acorn Coffee filled the large exterior hall, making Percy feel very out of place, as did the golden oak that covered almost every surface—from the floors, to the paneled walls, to the coffered ceiling overhead. At the vestibule's far end sat a long table covered in pastries and carafes of the Acorn beverage and cream and sugar. A few cups and saucers remained. He'd only imbibed the liquid once—when calling on his lumberjack client in the logging camp outside of town.

A board was angled toward two massive closed doors to the auditorium. *Catering Large Outdoor Events—Women's Society of Detroit* it pronounced.

He exhaled a long breath. What a conundrum.

Percy thumped his fingers against his hat. He drew Christian's scrawled missive from his pocket. Gratiot Hall was indeed the correct place. *Date correct.* He pulled his pocket watch out. *Time also correct.* If he'd come all this way and the event had been canceled, then perhaps there would be time to call on Miss Mott. But he'd not managed a pretext under which he could approach her. Perhaps he'd share what his client had chosen to do and that would open the door to other conversation.

Huffing a sigh, he checked the chalkboard once more—a futile attempt. The words would not have changed in the minute since he'd first scanned them.

On a nearby table, he located a leaflet and opened it. At the top, Miss Eugenie Mott was listed as the founder of the society and one of today's presenters. He frowned. How could such a refined young woman work in a hot kitchen with an apron tied over one of her expensive Worth ensembles? Might be amusing to see what she had to say on the subject matter, though.

He opened a door as quietly as he could and entered into the back of the auditorium. He chose a lone chair close by that was away from the main seating area. Women, some clutching children, occupied the other places. A quick headcount revealed that around fifty adults desired to learn more about this venture. A buzz of excitement echoed through the chamber.

The auditorium looked much as his father's Scottish hunting lodge did—decorated with wood everywhere one looked. A pang of sorrow shot through him. He and Father had been close, hunting often and fishing in England and Scotland. Father had promised he'd come to Canada to visit, but he never had come. *I miss him.* He missed his mother and brothers and sisters, too, but he'd never harbored any illusions that they would ever cross the pond to visit him once he left.

The door behind him creaked, and when he spied the late arrival, a stoop-shouldered woman who shuffled slowly forward, he rose and went to her. "I have a chair I can move closer to the others if you wish, madam."

Rheumy eyes met his as a smile cracked her lined face. "Thank you, young man, but no need to move the seat—I should be able to hear fine."

"Yes, madam." He took her arm.

She leaned heavily upon him until he helped her into the chair.

At the front of the room, movement caught his eye as a slender auburn-haired matron strode up the stairs and onto the platform and made an announcement about the privies. He stifled a laugh. But when Eugenie Mott, attired in a deep-plum day dress moved across the stage, he drew in a sharp breath. Even from this distance, her bearing and her handsome features made an impression. If anyone could speak of toilets and still appear regal, it was this woman.

Ahead of them, two ebony-haired women, dark woolen scarves tied loosely around their necks, pointed. "*Questa è lei - la nostra benefattrice.*"

Percy stiffened. What had they meant that Miss Mott was their benefactress? Or did they mean Mrs. Carrie Booth-Moore who now joined them on the dais? He recognized Booth-Moore from the Detroit social pages. Mrs. Booth-Moore was married to a well-known philanthropist. The women appeared completely at ease in front of the crowd—which wasn't meant to include him.

Dutch, Irish, French, and Scandinavian accents mingled as women remarked upon the ladies onstage. Detroit truly was a city of immigrants. Christian had, on more than one occasion, asked Percy to come and join him to translate conversations from German, French, and Italian clients. Having grown up with visitors from throughout Europe, and having been classically schooled, Percy had assumed all educated lawyers could translate documents and converse with their European-raised clients. But this catering group, save for a few, wore threadbare clothing and their countenances bore evidence of hard living, unlike his family's visitors and unlike the well-attired society ladies before them on stage.

Percy's paltry contributions to church funds were nothing compared to teaching a skill which could bring a new life. *Lord, what can I do to ease suffering for these women? Show me.*

A third lady joined them. If he was right, that was the legendary cook from the Empress Hotel. Mrs. Mulcahey was known on both sides of the water for her superior skills.

Eugenie nodded at Mrs. Mulcahey then stepped to the podium. "Good morning, ladies! I'm Eugenie Mott, and I wish to welcome you back to our continued training in the manner in which we might establish ourselves as…"

The beautiful woman's dark eyes met his and the connection coursed through him, like a cup of warm treacle syrup.

"That is…" Miss Mott cleared her throat, her cheeks visibly pink even from this far back in the auditorium.

Movement from the back of the auditorium caught Eugenie's eye, causing her to stutter. A tall dark-haired man in a navy tailcoat stood next to an elderly stranger, who was seated in a chair.

It was Mr. Gladstone. What was he doing there? And who was the woman with him?

Eugenie moistened her lips. She had to proceed regardless of whether the most handsome man she'd ever met happened to be standing right there, looking at her.

"As you know, we have procured a lease for the Alcott building."

A resounding cheer went up. She laughed and pressed a hand to her chest. "The old factory is the perfect site for us to practice our skills."

"Amen!"

"Yes, ma'am!"

"And this afternoon, Mrs. Mulcahey will spell out our agenda for our continuing classes."

She turned to whisper to Tara, "Please proceed while I go speak with the gentleman in the back."

"Yes indeed."

As Eugenie departed the stage, many eyes followed her, but Tara quickly began to recount what the women would be doing the next week as they mastered cooking and catering skills. Moving as quickly as she could, Eugenie soon found herself breathless. Surely it was her blasted corset being too tight and not because she was nearing the handsome Canadian attorney.

She tried to assume a politely interested expression and not stare at him with doe eyes. She leaned in so that she would not be overheard. "Mr. Gladstone, what brings you to my assembly?" Not exactly hers, but she felt the responsibility greatly.

He arched a dark eyebrow at her and leaned in. "This was supposed to be *my* event." Pleasant scents of evergreens and cinnamon cloaked him.

Heavens, I probably smell strongly of the Acorn Coffee we brewed earlier for our demonstration in economy. "I don't think so—I've had it booked for several months now."

Chuckling, he reached into his pocket and drew out what she recognized as a Canadian telegram and handed it to her. "Read for yourself, Miss Mott."

Eugenie scanned the message. "This is an error." Was he trying to annoy her?

The elderly lady, seated nearby gave Eugenie the sweetest little smile. She looked vaguely familiar, but this woman was not one of their regulars.

"No, this, I believe, is Christian's, or rather Mr. Zumbrun's attempt at a joke on me."

"A joke?" She looked from the strange woman and up into his smiling face. This close she could see the rim of navy in his gray-green eyes. *Such beautiful eyes.*

He leaned in. "Do you agree?" he whispered. His warm breath fanned her cheek and she took a step back.

She tried to keep her voice quiet. "I cannot say, sir." Weren't Englishmen supposed to be reserved? Mr. Gladstone was making her head swirl.

"If I were a betting man, I'd wager that's it." He crossed his arms over his broad chest. "Christian used to pull pranks on me when I first moved to Windsor, and now he's started it up again."

Were all attorneys so silly? Certainly not. And Mr. Zumbrun had always treated her and Father with the utmost decorum.

The older woman gazed up at the stage, where Tara was repeating the class schedule in French. A few other women, in the audience, were casting surreptitious glances in Eugenie's direction. She needed to get back up there and help. That's what she was here for, and these ladies were her mission in life.

"Regardless, I have an auditorium of women to tend to." She spun on her heel and made her way across the long room and back up toward the dais but paused at the bottom step.

She blinked a few times at the realization that she was mainly ornamental on that stage. Carrie would be speaking and then Tara again. All Eugenie had to do was offer a closing statement. Well, she'd make it a splendid speech. She sat on a bench at the bottom of the stage as the other women gave detailed instructions on catering etiquette and the preparation of the Acorn Coffee, artificial honey, and a substitute for cream. Eugenie made notes on a narrow tablet with a short pencil stub retrieved from the bottom of her reticule. She couldn't imagine that Mr. Zumbrun would deliberately send Mr. Gladstone to her event. Surely the handsome attorney would depart now that he'd been properly informed that this was an error. She chewed her lower lip, tempted to turn to see if the handsome man was yet there. What man would be so ridiculous as to listen to an hour of cooking lesson planning?

Some time later, both Tara and Carrie finished their instructions. Eugenie she joined her friends on the stage.

At the back of the auditorium stood Mr. Percival Gladstone, arms still crossed, leaning against the entryway looking for all the world as though he intended to remain. When he grinned at her, Eugenie's heart did a little flip and she averted her gaze, fumbling with her notes.

Miss Mott's passionate speech and her kindness toward the women reminded Percy of his mother's love for the villagers. Mother had always emphasized that as lady of the manor she must reach out to others. A sudden pang of homesickness threatened to overwhelm him. He continued to lean against the oak-encased entryway as casually as he could, watching Miss Mott. She'd given him a pointed look several times in the midst of her closing speech but he didn't leave.

When Miss Mott finished, to the ladies' applause, Percy went to the elderly woman he'd helped earlier. "Madam, allow me to assist you." He helped her to rise from the chair.

"Thank you, young man. Your mother must be proud of the son she raised."

His cheeks heated. *Was the Marchioness of Kent proud of her now-Canadian barrister son?* "Thank you, madam."

The stranger smelled faintly of cloves and peppermint, reminding him of his childhood nanny. She gave him a gentle smile. "Will you celebrate our Lord's birth with her this Christmas?"

What a strange way to put it. He stiffened. "I'm afraid not."

"But you'd like to?"

It was as though she'd read his mind. As an attorney, he often kept his face a blank slate. "I would, if only it could be possible."

She gave a low chuckle. "All things are possible. Especially at Christmastime."

Something about her words, and the way she said them, gave him pause. She gave him a slight nod as someone called his name.

Percy turned away as Eugenie Mott strode toward him, greeting several ladies as she moved, her cheeks flushed. He smiled in acknowledgement then looked back to see if the infirm woman, who'd struggled so hard to attend this meeting, required assistance. But she was gone. He turned and scanned the dozen or so women who were leaving. How had she departed so quickly?

"Mr. Gladstone?"

He swiveled around. "Yes?"

"You look as though you've seen a ghost."

He ran a hand through his hair. "Not quite. I was helping one of your attendees."

"I saw you. The last one in? The elderly woman you stood beside?"

"Yes."

"That was very kind." Miss Mott smiled up at him. "But I've never seen her before."

"She's not one of your ladies? Certainly acted like she was."

"No." Her dark eyebrows drew in, then quickly released. "Perhaps she simply wanted to come in from the street and the chill autumn air."

"No harm in that." Still, it was puzzling. But that wasn't why he'd tarried.

As they waited for the women to clear from the hall, Eugenie greeted most by name as they departed. Many eyed him with curious gazes.

When the auditorium doors closed in finality, Eugenie turned to him. "I think they've all departed."

He didn't want their conversation to end. "May I escort you home?"

"I'd planned on walking back." Eugenie stood straighter. "It's only a few blocks."

Did she not wish to spend time with him? "It was threatening to rain again, earlier."

"Yes." She dipped her chin.

Was this so difficult a decision? His courage threatened to leave. "Why don't I hail us a cab?"

She looked up at him, her features tense. "I could get my own."

"Why not drive together?" This independent woman intrigued him. "I can sweeten the ride with a donation to your charity. Would that convince you?" He offered what he hoped was a dashing smile—one his older brother, the heir, could pull off so convincingly.

She laughed softly. "I think I could tolerate you for the short distance to my home."

Chapter Four

I'm only tolerable?" Percy feigned distress.

"I'll contemplate that further while I fetch my coat and bonnet." She arched her eyebrows at him then strode off toward the row of hooks halfway up the room.

He couldn't help grinning. She had a heart to help others—as he did.

Before long, she rejoined him. "Mr. Gladstone, I cannot believe you sat through our presentation." She shook her head.

"I think it is admirable what you are trying to do for the Civil War widows."

"Thank you."

He opened the door for her. Soon he'd procured a taxi and they were on their way to the Mott home.

With the lovely woman seated close beside him, Percy had the sudden desire to cover her hand with his but refrained. "Have you always enjoyed cookery?" He had a hard time imagining her in a kitchen.

"No." She gave a curt laugh.

The carriage seemed to groan as they turned the street corner and onto a wide avenue. Eugenie clutched the seat as they rounded the curve.

"What prompted you to undertake your mission?

She sighed. "I've felt a nudging in my spirit to do something more important—something outside my social circle—ever since Pascal died."

"Who's Pascal?"

She averted her gaze. "He was a dear friend of mine. A childhood sweetheart. All of Detroit society presumed we'd marry when he returned from the war. But that never happened."

From the way she said her words, it was clear Pascal had died. "I'm sorry."

The carriage rolled on. A gas lighter raised his tall light to a street-side lamp. Darkness came early as they eased toward winter and would soon be upon them this night.

"It was a hard blow." She ducked her chin, her hat's velvet ribbons dangling against her creamy neck. "I considered what might have happened if we'd married and had children. What would that have been like? I know my life would have been so much harder."

Miss Mott didn't seem able to even use words that directly bespoke Pascal's death. Had she not recovered from the loss? "What made you accept Ontevreden, then?"

"That was my father's doing and I like, or rather liked, to keep him happy." She wiped away a tear. "I think Father must have known he didn't have much time left—at least that's what his physician said. My doctor didn't approve of Horace."

"Speaking of Mr. Ontevreden, I advised my client to end the courtship and she did."

"I haven't seen him nor heard anything of late about him." Eugenie nibbled her lower lip. "Horace wasn't supportive of my plans either. That was the thing I most regretted when I was considering marrying him to please my father."

"You really love this work, don't you?"

"I do. I love the idea of helping others help themselves. I've been involved in one way or another since Pascal died. So, just past five years now."

There. She'd said the word. *Died.* And five years earlier. Yet she may still mourn him.

The carriage rolled on over the macadam road, the horse's *clip-clopping* settling into a steady rhythm.

Miss Mott sighed. "About a third of my friends lost their sweethearts or husbands—if not through death, through severe injury or emotional distress that stole their loved ones away."

"A devastating toll. One many Canadians also shared, who'd decided to take up arms for the cause of freedom."

"Yes. So, if I can do something to soften the blows they've taken, I shall." She was so earnest, it touched him.

Percy tapped his fingers on his knee. "Those who've escaped slavery, they, too, suffer even now as they seek work." His housekeeper, gardener, cook, and stable hands had all come north to freedom. They deserved a good Christmas. He'd make sure they all had time off this year. He'd manage to get by alone, bachelor that he was.

"We have a handful of ladies in our group who made it to freedom yet had no skills with which to support themselves. So we teach them. And we have women who resorted to terrible things to keep themselves and their children alive after the war took their men."

Likely she meant women of ill repute. Had that prompted her father to seek to have her married? Perhaps he feared her social standing would suffer. The Motts were a revered family, according to Christian.

The carriage rolled to a stop.

Miss Mott's eyes widened and she cocked her head. "Perhaps you could help me with something instead of donating to my cause."

"How?"

To his surprise, she pressed her hand atop his. "Please come in and have tea with me, Mr. Gladstone."

"I'd be delighted."

She lifted her hand and he felt coolness where her warm touch had been. "I'd like to ask your advice about my plan to open some type of home where some of my ladies could live. There are a great many who sleep in the back rooms of shops or worse."

"It would be my pleasure to do what I can to help." Father had expressed to his eldest brother, the heir, that he was born to serve, to lead, and to offer aid to those who lived at their estate. But it had been Percy who'd taken those words to heart, about helping others.

29

"Pretty words for someone who'd insisted that boyish silliness had brought you to my lecture."

"But I mean them." An inspiration hit him. "Say, this may be a schoolboy prank in return, but what if we call upon Attorney Zumbrun at home and tell him we received *his invitation* to tea?"

She laughed. "His invitation? Which I take it was never issued?"

"Quite right." He tugged at his loose silk cravat.

"First let me apprise Lorena of where I'll be going. I don't want her and the staff to worry."

Might as well be bold. What could he lose? "Tell Miss Lorena that I'll be taking you to dinner as well."

Her tinkling laughter delighted him. "I must have forgotten about that invitation you sent. Perhaps lost—like Mr. Zumbrun's?"

"Just so." He chuckled.

Percy assisted Miss Mott from the carriage. She hurried inside, her skirts swaying to and fro as she crossed the herringboned brick path to the imposing home. He scanned the gardens, going fallow and, to the left, the rosebushes bearing clusters of rosehips. On the right, a tall oak, maple, and birch clustered together. Beneath the trees huddled evergreen shrubs and a holly bush that would soon bear fruit. Christmas truly would be here before they knew it.

When Percy was young, their estate gardener had allowed him to help with the Christmas greenery. Percy had spent the day, unbeknownst to his mother and father, cutting and wiring holly branches together. Cook had brought him every manner of beverage she was testing for the twelve days of celebration upcoming. Thankfully he'd sampled only small amounts of the eggnog, hot chocolate, spiced Russian tea, and the heavily creamed coffee that Cook had brought him. If he'd overindulged, Percy would have been ill and Mother would have learned about his doings. What happy memories.

He instructed the cab driver where to take them. The horses pawed at the road. "Calm down there you two rapscallions."

Soon, Miss Mott rejoined him and they made their way to the Zumbrun's three-story brownstone a quarter mile away. When

Percy, with Eugenie Mott on his arm, knocked on the door, it was Christian himself who opened it. Behind him, three of his four sons jumped on settees in the parlor. Zumbrun's daughter chased their hound up the hallway stairs.

Christian's wife, Jenny, fisted her hands and called out, "Stop! All of you!"

Only the dog seemed to have listened for he jumped down and ran back to his mistress.

Christian blinked at them several times. He exhaled a loud puff of air, bowed dramatically, and then waved them inside. "Guess I shouldn't be too surprised to see you here, Gladstone, should I?"

"Of course not." Percy waved the telegram in front of him as they entered. "I got your *invitation*, after all."

"Papa!" One of the boys ceased bouncing and ran toward them. "It's my gadfather!"

"Godfather, not gadfather." Christian pulled Matthew up into his arms.

Percy closed the door behind him.

"But he says 'egad' when I show him my drawings. So he's my gadfather," the boy insisted.

"I told you to not say that word." Jenny frowned at the child.

Christian set his son down again.

"He says it." The child jabbed a stubby finger at Percy's leg.

Percival's cheeks warmed. "I've been working on it, Matthew."

The boy raised his arms. "Touch the ceiling?"

"Of course." He picked up the child and raised him high overhead until little Matthew could touch the ceiling in the entryway.

The boy grinned and wrapped his arms around Percy's neck then planted a slobbery kiss on his cheek. "Got ya!"

"Indeed you have, young man." Percy lowered the imp to the floor then retrieved his handkerchief and wiped his face dry.

Christian cackled and mussed his son's tawny hair. "Good one, Mattie."

"Might even be a two-handkerchief one." Percy scowled at his friend. "You really shouldn't encourage him."

Miss Mott shook her head. "Perhaps you shouldn't be so gullible. It appears young Master Zumbrun has your number, Mr. Gladstone."

Jenny clutched the beagle as her daughter tried to pry him free. "Good to see you, P.!"

"Now don't start that." Percival held up his hands in surrender. The trio of boys now bouncing again happily in the parlor would begin their jokes if they heard their mother calling him "P."

Christian rubbed his nose. "Could have worse nicknames for you, I fear."

"Christian Zumbrun!" Jenny's fake outrage elicited a giggle from Eugenie.

Percy rocked on his heels. "Listen, we're on our way to dinner, so no need to worry about us staying, Jenny."

The pretty matron passed the hound to Christian. Percy leaned in and kissed her cheek, catching the scent of talcum and lemons.

"But I'm making lemon sponge cake."

One of his favorites. He chewed his lower lip. "We've got a cab waiting. Just wanted to say hello."

They made their farewells and were soon back in the snug carriage and on their way.

"They're so comfortable together." Miss Mott's voice held longing. "It reminds me of how my mother and father were."

"But without the many children."

"Yes, that was my mother's greatest sorrow—three little babes are buried in the church graveyard. I suppose I should put flowers on the graves, for Mother's sake, but. . ."

"I'm sorry."

"Don't get me wrong, my mother was a happy woman with a deep faith. But she'd have thrived having a household of children like the Zumbruns have."

"And you? Do you wish to have a house full of children?"

He heard her sharp intake of breath. What had made him ask such a deeply personal question?

"My dear Barrister Gladstone, was that the preliminary to a proposal of marriage or are you simply interrogating me?"

They both broke into comfortable laughter. "I apologize. I'm so accustomed to asking questions. I fear you're the victim of that habit I've acquired."

"It's all right. Yes, I do suppose I'd like to have a house full of happy laughter echoing from children who are well-loved."

Well-loved. He'd been well-loved. He'd known it. But the requirements of his station in life had weighed his father down. And his mother as well. The two were often busy but both had carved out time to spend with their children. Why, then, had Father not kept his promise to come see him?

She tapped his hand. "I give you leave to call me Eugenie."

He laughed. "And please call me Percy."

"Where are you taking me, Percy?" She leaned toward the window.

Ahead, on the right, sat the Waterview, a delightful inn where he stayed if he had prolonged business in Detroit. Anticipating possible business dining after the supposed "event," Percy had already procured a room. "The food here is excellent."

"Good friends of my family own this place." A frown skittered over Eugenie's brow. "Father brought me here once a month. He loved their roast beef."

"You must miss him."

"Dearly."

"I'm very sorry for your loss."

"Thank you. They say it gets easier with time, but I don't really believe that."

"I think grief changes over time. With God's help it becomes easier to bear, but that remnant is still there, like a shadow that pales but never completely disappears."

Over dinner, beneath the gaslight, Percy kept Eugenie talking about her childhood and shared about his, growing up in England.

"Are you truly the son of a duke?" Eugenie sipped her coffee.

"No, he's a marquess—which is below the rank of a duke." He was suddenly aware of the age and cut of his suit. His brother would be attired in the very latest fashion from London. "And I'm the fourth son, like little Matthew Zumbrun. I think that's why I've taken my godfather duties rather seriously."

"Do you have a deep faith?"

He eyed her over his uplifted cup of coffee. "I believe you have the makings of a barrister yourself, Miss Mott."

Her cup rattled as she abruptly set it in its saucer. "I'm sorry, excuse my forwardness."

He waved a hand as he set his own cup down gently. "Nothing to excuse you for. I was merely teasing, which I enjoy a great deal, I fear."

A low chuckle began before Eugenie gave a full-throated laugh, causing an elderly couple seated at a nearby table to glance in their direction. She raised her napkin to her rosebud mouth and patted it. "I believe you do enjoy teasing almost as much as your godson does."

He leaned in on his elbows, a bad habit his nanny had failed to drill out of him, and steepled his fingers together before him. "Well, I'm not jesting about this—I've experienced a splendid time with you this evening and I'd love to repeat dinner with you in Windsor sometime."

Her pretty face became somber. "I'm afraid I have far too many duties here between now and Christmas, with my ladies, to make any social appointments."

Appointments? He tried to hide his dismay. Perhaps all the conversation they'd had earlier in the dinner about her plans for housing had been like an appointment for her. He lifted a hand as casually as he could manage. "I've quite a few upcoming court cases I must prepare for as well. But should you require further assistance with your endeavor, please contact me." He retrieved a calling card from the sterling silver case his brother had gifted him with upon his graduation from Oxford.

She accepted the card and her lips parted as though she were about to say something. She slipped the card into her bag.

"Well, then. Let's have the doorman call the cab for you, Miss Mott." Why had he thought that an American socialite would have any interest in him other than for business advice? Well, he wasn't going to simply lie down and roll over like the Zumbrun's hound had been trained to do. "But I insist on accompanying you home and making sure you're safely inside."

A smile tugged at the corner of her lips. "I don't suppose you come to Detroit often for business matters, do you, Mr. Gladstone?"

"I do now." He placed his hand atop hers and left it there. When she didn't pull away, his shoulders relaxed. "Would you object to me being your unofficial business advisor on the home purchase?"

Never mind that real estate purchases were well outside his purview normally.

"Are you donating your services, sir?"

"I am."

"Then on behalf of the board, I accept."

He pulled his appointment calendar from his inside coat pocket and his pencil. "How about we meet again in a few days?"

She nibbled her lower lip. "Can you join us at our new building, the Alcott, midday, during our break?"

"Splendid." For the first time in a long time, hopeful expectation rose in him like a flame sputtering to life in a trimmed-too-short candle.

Chapter Five

Windsor, Ontario

*R*ain tip-tapped at Percy's mullioned windowpanes, as if demanding entrance to his cozy office. With coals burning in the grate, a hot mug of gunpowder tea with honey before him, and two inquiries already addressed, Percy wasn't about to be concerned with the pattering of raindrops. Surely it would cease before he joined Eugenie for the Scott's Theater production that evening. Twice more he'd gone to Detroit to visit with Miss Mott for "business" consultations—purely legal advice on her end, perhaps, but of a more romantic nature on his. Hopefully it wasn't his imagination that she was softening toward him.

A light knock on his office door brought him back to the reality of who he was—a small-time barrister in a tiny Canadian town with nothing to commend him as anything other than an advisor to the beautiful woman.

"Come in!"

"Cable for you, sir." Percy's assistant handed him the telegram. What an amazing invention—wiring messages across the ocean, something his uncle had been involved with on the English side of the ocean.

When Antoine left, Percy read the message.

Maidstone, England

P, Arrive Windsor 23 December Love M

"What?" He dropped the message onto his desk blotter. Hopefully his mother had also sent a letter outlining when and who all were arriving. He needed specifics—he was a man who required details, and well she knew it.

He'd only just that morning given his staff early Christmas bonuses and time off for the holidays. He couldn't rescind it. He wouldn't. But oh, this was joyous news, too!

Percy got up and went to the door and called to Antoine, "I need some help."

"Yes, sir?"

"I need a list of all the servants in Windsor who might be available for Christmas work."

His clerk's face pulled into a frown. "Are your servants not sufficient?"

"I told Venus, Sabina, and Lemrich that they have the entire holiday season off. They've been wanting to visit their relatives in Ohio." His houseman, Scipio, would remain.

"Are you not a bachelor?"

Percy braced himself against the door. "My mother sent me a rather cryptic message that I have company coming for Christmas."

Antoine's dark eyebrows into an inverted V. "You've put yourself into a *difficile désordre* then, I fear."

A difficult mess. "Why is that?"

"Because you can't simply go out and find *Noel* workers. It's not like right after the war. People have…" Antoine looked upward at the wood-paneled ceiling, one of his habits when searching for the right words. "*Se sont établis.* They've become established already in a household, like your workers."

"Do you have any suggestions?"

"*Certainement.*" He gestured west. "Put them up in Hotel Cadotte on the river."

"In Detroit? I can't do that." He certainly couldn't afford it, not on his earnings. They'd likely stay several weeks after traveling so far. "And don't you mean *L'hotel Cadotte*?" He couldn't resist the tease.

"I sometimes forget my French, sir, with your insistence on English. *Merci,* for the reminder!"

Percy shrugged playfully. "No trouble at all."

Antoine rubbed his short goatee. "As far as the requests, I'll do my best, sir. But no *promesses*."

"Thank you. Oh, and I'll need the best figgy pudding you can find."

"But with no actual figs, *oui*?" Antoine jested about this every year.

"*Non, monsieur*. No figs in my figgy pudding." Raisins were used, not figs. "And while you're out, please ask the *patisserie* to put up several Queen's cakes and fruitcakes for me for Christmas." The bakery's fruitcakes required weeks of soaking and preparation, so he'd best get on the list.

Panic threatened to rob his focus. He had to get his work accomplished so that he might spend time with his family when they arrived. And he needed to set up a hunting expedition for Father. And get reservations for musical entertainment for Mother.

His trip to Detroit might need to be sooner, rather than later, today.

Antoine cleared his throat. "Will that be all, sir?"

"Yes, for now. If I'm not here when you return, I'll have departed for Detroit."

"Again?" The way Antoine drew out the word suggested frustration.

Heat coursed up Percy's neck and settled in his cheeks. "I have a social engagement."

The younger man shrugged. "Even a lowly *légiste* such as myself knows you haven't brought in your evening clothes for no reason." Antoine inclined his head toward the wooden hanging valet in the corner, upon which hung Percy's dinner attire.

"You're no lowly law clerk. You're talented, and I don't know what I'd do without you."

"*Merci*."

Percy cleared his throat. "Not all of my activities in Detroit are personal. I also must take care of some business there."

"*Certainement*. I'll make sure everything is in order for tomorrow morning's case."

"Thank you. And while I'm in Detroit, I'll ask a friend..." Never mind that it was the woman who was far more than a friend. "If they know of any workers who might be available."

Antoine tapped the side of his head. "Good thinking, Monsieur Gladstone."

Especially if it meant he got to spend more time with Detroit's most beautiful lady. And if he encountered the elderly lady he'd assisted at Eugenie's seminar, he'd tell her that she was right.

Anything was possible at Christmastime.

Eugenie smoothed her black satin skirt and examined her reflection in the looking glass. Perhaps satin was too gaudy for mourning. But Father would have approved. Would Percy? She picked up her long jet and silver earrings from her cherry bureau that flanked the highboy in her room. She screwed the back onto the first one, and tugged. It was safely attached. Then she repeated the procedure with the other earring.

"Miss Mott?" Lorena's voice trembled. "Would you take a look at my dress?"

Standing in the doorway, attired in a new deep-green damask ensemble that enhanced her hazel eyes, her maid appeared younger than Eugenie had thought her to be. "You look lovely."

She cast her eyes downward. "Thank you, ma'am."

"Your sister and her family will be delighted to see you." At least Eugenie hoped so. The theater troupe members had sent only a brief note back, acknowledging their receipt of her servant's note.

"I should have let Angelina know I was alive." Lorena nibbled on her lower lip. "I don't blame her if she's angry."

"With the extra tickets that the theater gave us, several of my ladies are attending, too."

"You know some of them ladies, they're more than a little down on their luck—if you catch my meaning."

Eugenie raised a hand to cut her off. Some of her ladies were widows without any source of support while others had been enslaved or street ladies. Eugenie didn't want to hear it. "They've got a second chance, Lorena, and from here on out they'll be ladies. Ladies who conduct themselves accordingly and who help cater many a fancy event in Detroit society."

"Yes, ma'am, it's just…."

"I didn't take you for a snob, Lorena."

"No, ma'am, it's not me, it's the society people you takin' them out to work for. Some of them, well the men, they might recognize a few of them gals."

Eugenie sucked in a breath. She truly was as naïve as Horace always said. Look how foolish she'd been about him—about to marry him for her father's peace of mind. "You have a point. But hopefully with no makeup, no titian hair, and plain clothing, they'll fit in." She hoped. She prayed they would.

Before long, Eugenie's driver had transported them to the opera house. Lorena shared her concerns that with Angelina and her children apparently "passing" as white, perhaps the sisters' relationship should be kept secret. Angelina, whose father was white, unlike Lorena's, was only one-eighth of African descent. Angelina had been freed from slavery years before Lorena had escaped. Lorena, however, had been believed dead. What a happy discovery for Angelina to learn her sister had survived, but some guilt on Lorena's part.

Eugenie and Lorena arrived at the theater just as a clock chimed the half hour. That gave them a half hour before the performance. They descended the staircase, the scent of warm ham wafting up.

"That do smell good." Lorena smiled as they joined the catering crew downstairs where the reception had been set up. "But my nerves too on edge to enjoy any of this food tonight."

"We'll have to trust in God. Surely your sister will be glad to see you alive."

Something about the way her servant mumbled, "Umhum," disturbed Eugenie, but they were too close to all the workers to pursue this conversation. With Angelina and her children "passing" for white, their reunion was a tricky one for both. Eugenie prayed the sisters could work out their difficulties.

"I pray so." Lorena drew in a deep breath. "After the performance, I think I best go to the players' backrooms, Miss Mott, and see my sister."

"That might be best." Eugenie squeezed her servant's hand. "You'll have some privacy there." Unspoken, but implied, was that if Angelina and her family chose not to acknowledge Lorena as kin, then she'd not be joining in the reception.

Lorena departed. She'd be seated in the back section of the theater, despite being a family member of the Scotts. It was a shame, but there was nothing Eugenie could do about the theater's policies.

Laughter from nearby brought Eugenie's attention back to her task at hand. The ladies had outdone themselves in transforming the utilitarian basement into a welcoming space for the reception. Linens lent by Carrie covered the four long tables. Tara had loaned three sets of china from her first two marriages and one from her mother. Silver shone in baskets lined with pale blue napkins. Crystal goblets and decanters occupied one of the tables featuring a massive silver-plated bowl retrieved from the Mott's attic—one Mother had never used.

Nearby, Tara placed sugar-glazed berries atop a five-layer cake. "It's all ready. Now, you go back upstairs and find that handsome attorney who was here looking for you."

"Mr. Zumbrun?" Eugenie feigned surprise. "Why, he's already married, Mrs. Mulcahey."

Her friend laughed. "And well I know, as he's married to my cousin."

"So you must mean Mr. Gladstone has arrived."

Tara glanced past Eugenie.

"I have been seeking you out most desperately, Miss Mott." Percy's deep voice held a tease.

She swiveled to face him. "Most desperately?"

"Indeed." He pointed to the cake. "Mrs. Booth-Moore informed me I'm not to touch the ladies' creation until later, but how might I offer my expert opinion if I'm not allowed a taste?"

Tara's throaty laugh started Eugenie giggling. Her friend moved beside her. "You'll just have to imagine, Mr. Gladstone."

Eugenie cocked her head at him and gazed up at his handsome face. "You've got some creativity in that lawyerly brain of yours, haven't you?"

His lips pulled in. "Creative ways to steal a bite, perhaps."

She shook her head.

Percy extended his arm. "Shall we go upstairs before I am tempted to put my plan into action?"

Tara's eyes widened. "You make the action sound positively sinful."

"Which it is." Eugenie wagged a finger at Percy and laughed. "Touch that cake before the party and you'll have all of us ladies to answer to, and don't forget it!"

"Yes, ma'am." He made a show of bowing and clicking his heels together before he offered his arm.

They went upstairs and found their seats in the front semi-circle.

"I think I've found another place for your ladies to cater." He shifted in the velvet-upholstered seat.

"You have? Where is it?" Some of the women suffered from a very real desperation, unlike Percy.

"My family is coming from England—" A crease formed on his forehead.

"How wonderful." Was it really? Would she then be alone this year? She'd hoped to invite him for dinner.

"And I could use some help." His lips twisted, as though discussing the need was distasteful.

"What about your staff? I thought you had several workers." Eugenie adjusted her skirt.

"I've given them leave to travel to visit with family in Ohio."

"I see. I take it that was before you'd heard from your parents."

"From my mother, actually, but yes, quite right." He angled his body toward her and leaned in.

"I can check with my ladies and see if some can help." There were some who'd welcome a change of pace from the squalid conditions they lived in. "Might they stay at your home?"

"Yes." He named the compensation, which was generous. "And I have two upstairs attic rooms they could share."

The theater manager stepped up onto the dais. "And now I present, The Scott Family Players performing *The Wiclow Wedding*."

The curtains parted and soon, Eugenie was swept up in the play, filled with dramatic turns and romance. But she never forgot who was seated beside her and the wonderful way he made her feel.

She had to stop acting as if theirs was merely a business friendship.

But how? Especially if she was to have her ladies work for him. She mustn't let her feelings sway her.

Eugenie had much work yet to accomplish. She'd not let her ladies down.

Chapter Six

Sabina stood at the center of Percy's mahogany dining table, waving a wooden spoon in the air like a scepter. "I won't have anyone messing up my kitchen, now, ya hear, Mr. Gladstone?"

"I hear you." Percy wiped at his mouth with his napkin. "And as I just explained, Miss Mott will assemble a group of ladies who will take over the household duties while you are out."

"Humph!" Sabina crossed her arms. "If I'd a knowed your Ma and Pa and kin were comin', I'd not have told my folk I'd be acomin' to visit."

"It's all right." Percy set his napkin on the table and pushed aside his breakfast plate. "I'll instruct them that the kitchen must be returned to its original pristine condition before they leave."

"Prissy?" Her dark eyes widened. "My kitchen be so clean you coulda et your eggs off'n that floor in there."

"Pristine. It means 'immaculate.'"

When her face remained skeptical, he added, "Extremely clean to the point of perfection."

"'Zactly. My kitchen is in perfect condition, so don't let them ruin it."

"I won't."

Sabina took Percy's dirty utensils and placed them on the plate, and the napkin atop and stomped off to the kitchen. Percy exhaled in exasperation. This was becoming far more difficult than he'd imagined. He was sorely tempted to threaten Sabina that he'd find an Irish girl to replace her—that's what Christian's wife did whenever their servants made demands. Although Percy would never do that to poor Sabina. She'd suffered enough in one lifetime. But he could have a little more backbone, as his mother always said about him. Strange how he could be so commanding and demanding in court, but when it came to the people who he dealt with on a daily basis he was more kitten than tiger. Probably because of constantly placating his older brothers as he was growing up and looking for affection and approval wherever he could find it.

He ran his thumb over his lower lip, recalling how close he had come to kissing Eugenie goodnight after the cast party had ended.

His houseman, Scipio, who was in his twenties, shuffled into the room. His master in South Carolina had cut Scipio's ankles when he'd run away, leaving the young man with limited ability to walk. "Post arrived, sir."

"Thank you." He accepted the proffered missive, which Scipio had already slit open with the envelope knife. No fear of him reading Percy's message—all of his servants were receiving tutelage in reading and writing but were yet working on basic skills.

Mother's even-handed script flowed across the paper. Percy inhaled a steadying breath as he read of all the people his mother intended to bring with her. Father wasn't mentioned, but the new Earl of Cheatham, Barden Granville IV, and his wife would be accompanying her.

He set the missive down, his knuckles rapping the tabletop. He liked Barden a great deal—had attended university with him, where Bard was great fun. But he'd never met his wife, whom his mother indicated was an American, named Caroline. Furthermore, Mother inquired if Caroline's sister Deannamight also be allowed to stay at the spacious home he'd described in his letters.

Yes, the six-bedroom home was spacious for a bachelor with a staff of three, but with so many visitors how could he accommodate them all? And it was quite unlike his mother to invite others into someone else's home. No mention at all of Father. He exhaled and frowned. Perhaps she'd simply not thought to say. Not only that, but Bard was a third son. Was Mother confused?

He read rest of the letter carefully.

I thought you should know, that Lord Cheatham succumbed to a heart ailment. Soon after, his son and heir, Peter contracted pneumonia and perished. The second Granville son died from the London cholera epidemic.

So that was it. Percy exhaled a breath and dropped the letter to the table. *Oh my heavens.* His poor friend, Barden. That was too much, even for a clergyman like Bard, to contend with. Barden needed help and Percy would do what he could to bring some comfort this Christmas. But Percy needed more assistance, too, with a full house.

Seven years of Christmastide on his own. He covered the letter with his hand. He'd enjoy their presence to the fullest and not get bogged down in the "how" of *how* everything happened. God would provide. Yes, he'd have to do his bit, but surely the Lord wouldn't send these riches of family and friends unless He had a plan.

Bard had led Percy to the Lord while they were school chums. This was his chance to bless him in return and allow the new Lord and Lady Cheatham to lean on him if needed.

As Eugenie prepared to leave for the practice kitchens, she eyed the empty mail salver, the silver reflecting beneath the gaslight of the parlor. Father had disclosed that many of his friends disapproved of her social "do-gooding." Could that be the reason she'd received no Christmas invitations, or was it because she was in mourning? But surely someone would have extended her a Christmas invitation. Yet none had arrived.

Christmas will be a lonely one. Percy would be busy with his family. Last night when she thought he was going to kiss her, she'd almost raised up on her tiptoes to accept the press of his mouth on hers. Thank goodness she hadn't, or how embarrassed she'd be now.

She retrieved her velvet-trimmed coat and matching bonnet from the pegs along the wall and headed to the front where the carriage awaited. After a short ride her driver pulled up by the imposing old factory building. Despite the chill, warmth suffused her. This was really happening. Ahead, a dozen of her ladies entered the building.

She could spy Carrie Booth-Moore from afar, a brilliant red plume on her hat bobbing as she strode toward the entrance—the picture of confident womanhood. A little of her friend's self-assurance had waned recently, when Carrie learned that her mother-in-law was coming to stay with them for the holidays. Carrie had informed Eugenie that she'd have to reduce instruction time.

Eugenie exhaled, her breath forming a billowing puff in the chill morning air. Winter was knocking at the door. But were they ready to answer?

Once inside, Eugenie hung her coat beside those ranging from Tara's elegant fox-trimmed cape to a garment so thin that a white handkerchief could be seen through the threadbare front pocket. Eugenie sighed. They were offering these women real skills that could help them overcome their poverty.

It was like that saying— *Teach a man a fish...* Only in this case, it was *Train a lady to make a delicious sugarplum recipe...*

"Excuse me, Miss Mott." A dark-haired girl perhaps thirteen or so, the daughter of one of their trainees, Mrs. Fox, stepped toward her. Both she and her mother dressed surprisingly well in comparison with most of their students.

"Yes?" What was Mrs. Fox's child's name? *Ada.* "How can I help you, Ada?"

The girl smiled tremulously. "Actually, I prefer to be called Adelaide, if you don't mind."

"Certainly." Why didn't the mother call her Adelaide? Regardless, it was no difficulty to call her by her preferred appellation.

"My mother is unwell but wished that I sit in on tonight's lesson."

Eugenie couldn't help frowning. Mrs. Fox needed to master all of the skills. "Much of what we do is actually prepare the food or 'hands on' work, and you're not enrolled."

Adelaide averted her gaze. "Yes, ma'am, but I came prepared to take notes." She pulled a notepad and pencil from her small cloth pouch.

"That would be fine, then. There's a stool right in the corner, where you can sit and watch."

"Thank you, ma'am." The girl's wan face lit up.

Eugenie half-expected the girl to skip into the building. Instead, Adelaide, head held high, marched into the room and took her spot in the corner. What was it her mother said the child was fascinated by? *Numbers.* She'd said that if they ever needing help with bookkeeping that her daughter was a genius with numbers. But didn't every parent think their child or children were especially gifted? Mother had certainly believed Eugenie was a great beauty and that was far from the truth. She was average. Perhaps a smidge above. Who knew what skill young Adelaide actually possessed when it came to numbers and the like.

Tara strode to the center of the room. She stood on an upside-down wooden crate and clapped her hands. "We're all working together today on traditional Christmas recipes, so gather round."

After the ladies had received instruction on preparing sugarplums, Carrie, Tara, and Eugenie sampled the shortbread cookies that had been baked and tinned the previous day.

Carrie quirked a dark eyebrow. "Delicious!"

Wiping a crumb from the edge of her mouth, Tara grinned. "Yes."

Eugenie savored the sweet buttery taste. "Perfection. And look how everyone is keen to master their own version of the perfect sugarplum recipe.

"We still need to come up with a name for our catering group." Carrie sighed. "My husband says that in business one must have a catchy name.

"Where I work, I'm just glad they don't call me something profane." Tara chuckled.

"Sugarplum Ladies." Eugenie raised her hand high. "The Sugarplum Ladies."

Tara frowned. "That's what you want to call them?"

"It sounds a bit too Christmasy." Carrie cocked her head. "But you know, it would kind of go with that expression about things being plummy or good."

"Yes. Sweet and good. That's our Sugarplum Ladies."

"Glad we got that sorted." Tara chuckled. "I'm going to go do some oversight."

Work continued, with a short break for lunch, followed by another lesson and demonstration.

"They're really mastering the skills, Eugenie." Carrie beamed like a proud mother.

Tara rang the bell to announce day's end.

As they began cleaning up, Eugenie grabbed the sturdy wood box and stepped up onto it. "I need to make an announcement. Actually, three of them."

The women stopped what they were doing. All eyes focused on Eugenie.

She surveyed the group. More could be safely housed. Warmth flowed through her. "First, we have secured a contract on a new building for those requiring housing!"

Some ladies gasped, a few began to cry, but most clapped loudly. When they quieted, Eugenie scanned the room. How many could help Percy? "Mr. Gladstone, the attorney who has been assisting us, at no cost may I add, is in need of household staff for Christmas. Might there be a few of you ladies who could help him out?"

A number of women stiffened. Had she offended? "There will be generous payment. Just remain behind for a few minutes and let me know. Thank you."

"And finally, I'd like to call our catering group The Sugarplum Ladies."

Murmurs began and then her ladies began to clap, until all had joined them.

When no one moved to leave, she added, "You're all dismissed for the day!"

How many would come forward to volunteer for Percy? Asking someone to help out for a few days during such an important time of year might prove difficult. As the other ladies streamed out, only a handful remained behind.

Eugenie quickly took a mental inventory of these ladies' strengths. Deborah set the prettiest tables and worked magic on all manner of vegetables and fruits. Melissa could coax the toughest piece of meat into tender submission and possessed leadership skills. Nancy's soups, consommés, and stews were unparalleled. Tina was happiest tidying up after everyone else but was also becoming accomplished with pastries.

Kathleen preferred staffing the tea and coffee carts. She had a heart for service to others and enjoyed being directly in contact with patrons. She also possessed a strong disposition of her worth in Christ and wouldn't be cowed by Percy's aristocratic parents if they were of the difficult sort—which Eugenie prayed they'd not be.

Kathleen finished cleaning up from the Russian tea she'd practiced preparing. She removed her apron and joined Eugenie and Carrie. "I'll be alone this Christmas, so I'd be happy for work."

Melissa moved toward them. "Kathleen and I are sharing a room above the mercantile and we're told they'd don't plan to heat the building Christmas Eve nor on Christmas Day."

Eugenie gasped. "Alone and with no heat?"

"How terrible. We can't have that." Tara scowled. "That man should be whipped."

Carrie's face displayed her shock at their friend's outburst. "Perhaps just a simple boycott of his business will do?" She tapped Tara's arm gently.

Shoulders raising and lowering with her sigh, Deborah stopped folding linens nearby. "My employer is doing the same."

"That's outrageous!" Tara's voice rose again.

Tina stepped forward. "This will give us a chance to earn our keep." She eyed the other women. "We've been talking, and we won't take charity."

"We need our pride." Melissa pinched a torn piece of her skirt between her long fingers.

"Last week's catering event paid off my rent with enough left over to pay some toward renting my room at the new building." Deborah removed her apron.

Carrie's dark eyes shone with approval as she smiled at each lady in turn.

Nancy covered the leek consommé she'd prepared. "My sons are both stationed at forts in Texas and won't be coming home. I'd be glad to help."

"How long does Mr. Gladstone need us?" Deborah exchanged a glance with Melissa. "We signed up for an extra cleaning job for after Christmas."

Eugenie tapped her toe. "A good question. I think he'd appreciate having help for about a week, when I imagine his household help will return."

"I can go for a week." Tina smiled. "I hope he's as generous as you say."

Eugenie told them the rate Percy had offered to pay her ladies. All were quiet for a moment, eyebrows raised. "His parents are the Marquess and Marchioness of Kent."

"Oh my." Nancy's shoulders slumped. "I don't know if I'm up to cooking for the likes of that."

Eugenie leaned toward her. "I'd not have asked if Carrie, Tara, and I didn't think you were ready. Besides, Mr. Gladstone is a barrister in a small town. I imagine he's expecting a little more simple fare." But was he? Eugenie nibbled her lower lip.

Kathleen's eyebrows drew together. "Will you be staying to help us?"

Maybe she should remain in Windsor with the volunteers. Her heart leapt at the prospect, but she'd not get ahead of herself. "We'll have to work out all the details and I'll let you know."

Movement in the corner caught her eye. Young Adelaide rose, stuffed her notepad in her reticule, and walked over to join Eugenie.

"If you have need of another, I'd be happy to help your Canadian friend."

"Won't your mother wish for you to be with her this Christmas?"

The girl locked eyes with Eugenie, and she could almost see the depths of sadness there. "I believe my mother would wish for me to help in any way I could."

Eugenie nodded. "Have her send me a note with permission. And are you averse to performing kitchen cleanup and the like? Can you follow simple directions from the other ladies?"

"Yes, ma'am. I mean, no, I'm not too proud to clean and to obey orders. And I shall procure a note from Mother for you."

"Fine. Send that to my home."

Soon, they'd both donned their coats, hats, and gloves and departed. Adelaide headed toward the nearby boarding house where she lived with her mother. *Dear God, help her get well soon.*

A handful of ladies and a girl. Could they pull off this event? And what were they getting into?

On her carriage ride home, Eugenie berated herself for not getting more information from Percy about his Christmas preparations. She'd see him soon for the opera on the Canadian side on Saturday. A touring company, with several members from eastern and northern Ontario, were bringing their production through before Christmas, enroute to visit family.

When she stepped into the house, the scent of roast beef enveloped her like a comforting hug. Would Percy's family enjoy roasts? Or would they prefer fancier fare like standing rib roast? Menus danced through her head as she considered several upcoming events the ladies were catering. A railroad executive had asked for a feast featuring only seafood, no meats, with a seven-course meal for fifty people at his estate outside of town, on the river. She removed her hat and set it on the wooden rack by the door.

Her butler, Mr. Morgan, came and took her coat. "Welcome home, miss."

"Thank you."

"You have a letter from Mrs. Swaine."

"Indeed? How delightful." Her spirits rose. How she loved this special woman. The Swaines owned substantial properties on Mackinac Island as well as a hotel in Detroit. It would be lovely to have Jacqueline Cadotte Swaine, one of her mother's closest friends, visit again sometime. How Eugenie loved to hear the stories of Mother and Jacqueline's times together.

Mr. Morgan cleared his throat. "It's a shame poor Mrs. Swaine lost those two sons during the war. They were both gracious young men."

She lowered her head. "Yes, they were." While it was rumored that her eldest son had fought for the South, no one spoke of it. "I can only pray that Jacqueline's little boy, Robert, brings her comfort." He must be toddling around by now.

Eugenie raised her head and met the servant's gaze. She swiped at a tear. Mr. Morgan, too, had a sheen in his eyes. Those young men had been right here in this home, visiting, not a decade earlier.

"She will always feel the loss, though, I believe." Mr. Morgan, like Eugenie, had known his own share of bereavements.

She drew in a breath. "I fear you are correct. Even so, I hope little Robbie helps soothe the hurt."

Mr. Morgan nodded.

"Could you bring the missive to me in the parlor? And send Lorena with some tea."

"Certainly, miss."

Eugenie eyed the Morris chair that Father had brought back from England the previous Christmas. With darkly stained wood, including the spindles, and beautifully artful fabric for the heavily padded seat and back, it was a bit of an oddity in the parlor. Eugenie had originally protested the piece's placement there but considering the comfort it gave with the ability to recline, surely this unusual style would someday catch on. Until then, she had to endure visitors' comments. But not tonight, and apparently not during the holidays. She pulled the ottoman close and sat down, removed her shoes, reclined slightly, and propped her feet up. Mother would have scolded and Father would have rolled his eyes.

Unexpected tears trickled down her cheeks. How she missed them. Her first Christmas all alone in this big house. Percy had his family coming and her ladies would be there working while she was on this side of the water, alone. Yes, she was falling in love with him, and yes, he seemed to care for her, too. But surely it was too soon for her to meet his family. Besides, she was in mourning for her father. But her Sugarplum Ladies needed her—didn't they?

She exhaled a huge sigh as Lorena entered the room with the tea cart and the letter. Eugenie inhaled the scent of orange, pekoe, and bergamot as her servant poured her tea.

Lorena passed her the envelope. "Mr. Morgan say to give you this."

"Thank you."

Lorena placed the teacup and saucer on the cherry side table next to her. Mother's and Father's tintype image beamed up at her from a nearby silver frame on the table.

Eugenie slit the envelope open and began to read the message.

My dearest Eugenie,

I apologize at my tardiness in sending this letter. I'd forgotten how busy life can be with two-year-old boys in the house! Robert continues to thrive and is a joy to us all. Perhaps not to his older sister, but perhaps she reveled a tad too much in being the baby of the family.

Lorena, who'd remained in the room, shifted from side-to-side. "Miss Mott, I got a favor to ask."

Eugenie looked up. "Yes?"

Concern crinkled Lorena's brow. "It's just that, well, my family is going to be coming back to visit with me."

"The Scotts?" Lorena hadn't mentioned having any other living family members.

"Yes, ma'am, and Mrs. Roat, be with them. She was like a second mother to my sister."

The two half-sisters had been separated when Mrs. Wilda Roat bought Angelina's freedom and taught her the trade of seamstress work. "That's a blessing." Yet Angelina Scott's older sister Lorena had remained enslaved until she'd escaped North.

"I was wonderin' if I might have a few days off from workin'?"

"Of course! I'm excited that you got to reconnect with your family."

"I don't know 'zactly when they comin. They lookin' for a place to stay."

This house would be almost empty. Eugenie wouldn't be like the uncharitable protagonist in Charles Dickens's recent story. "Lorena, why don't you ask them to stay here? The third floor has two smaller rooms for Julian and Charity, and I have two more rooms on the other end of the second floor that they're welcome to use."

Lorena's pretty features froze. "You mean that, ma'am?"

Eugenie sipped her tea and set the cup back on the saucer. "I think it would be delightful. And you can order all the garlands and what-nots that Mother used to have to make the place festive."

"Even with you in mourning, Miss Mott?" There was no censure in her servant's voice, just concern.

Surely by now Lorena should know that Eugenie didn't follow all social conventions. More than that, she wished to be of service to God and His people. "Would not even the bereaved invite the Christ child in?"

"Yes'm, I'm guessin' they would."

"So shall we. Feel free to have Mr. Morgan help you bring out the decorations at the appropriate time. Plan some dinners just for yourselves, too, and I'll gladly pay the expenses."

Lorena began to cry. She reached into her apron for a handkerchief and gently blew her nose. "You too good to me, miss."

"Every good thing we have comes from God. I thank Him we can offer shelter to your family."

She sniffed. Thank you." And if you don't mind me sayin', ma'am, I believe the good Lord may have brought Mr. Gladstone to you, for your good."

"I pray you're right. He certainly seems to enjoy helping others."

"That old Mr. Horace was a bad man. I near 'bout wore my knees out tryin' to pray him outta your life."

Eugenie dipped her chin.

Lorena tugged at her apron and left the room.
Eugenie lifted the letter again, to continue reading.

We will be arriving from up North near Christmas and will be at our hotel much of the time. We would very much enjoy a visit with you, wherever that might be.

Eugenie took a deep breath. What if that happened to be in Windsor? She simply couldn't miss seeing dear Jacqueline, her husband, and their two children, if at all possible.

You are welcome to stay at the hotel with us over the holidays, Jacqueline wrote.

Tears pricked Eugenie's eyes again. It was good to be asked.

Dearest Eugenie, I hate to ask you this, but I am in much need of a referral to an attorney who is known for his utmost discretion. I have some things I must put into place. Your father no doubt was vigilant in ensuring that his estate and businesses passed hands with no disruption and I wish to get sound advice for myself.

Oh my, this sounded serious. Jacqueline was correct about Father leaving her well-situated and his businesses in order. Mother would have wanted Eugenie to help her dear friend. She pressed the missive to her chest. There was no other attorney Eugenie would trust so much as Percy Gladstone.

This Christmas was becoming more complicated by the moment.

But with Christ in it all—Eugenie knew that God's grace would carry her through.

Chapter Seven

*P*ercy crossed out the previous day's date on the calendar atop his blotter. How could only one day spent without seeing Eugenie Mott seem more like a week? She'd been busy with training activities for her ladies and in all the associated activities involved.

A grim-faced Antoine rapped on the open door and strode to the desk. He passed his notepad to Percy. "I've procured a carriage driver, footman, lady's maid, chamber maid, handyman, and *un garçon* to run errands—but no cook nor kitchen servants."

"I don't need an errand boy." Percy exhaled a breath and set the notepad down on his desk, scanning the names, recognizing one in particular. "The lady's maid has served time for, ahem, soliciting, so she's out."

Antoine coughed, his cheeks red. "Sorry, sir."

"The chambermaid's name is also familiar for the same offense." He lifted his pen from the inkwell and crossed out the two names.

"Most of the extra service help in town, *les cuisiniers et leurs aides,* were already contracted from the previous year."

"I've asked Miss Mott if any of her ladies might do the duties." Hopefully Eugenie could supply the cooks and their helpers.

"It is so late to be inquiring, sir."

"Yes, well, this visit was rather unexpected."

"But a welcome one, *n'est ce pas*?"

"Yes, very welcome. I'll ask Miss Mott, when I take her to the opera, if she might have found some American women who can help."

"Speaking of which, you might wish to return home and *préparez-vous pour ce soir*, sir."

Percy pulled his watch from his vest and checked the time. Perhaps he'd best go and prepare for the evening.

Now, hours later, he was glad that he'd taken Antoine's advice. The ferry arrived just as his carriage driver had pulled into a spot at the wharf. Eugenie was about to arrive on Canadian soil. *On my side of the water.*

Once the boat was secured at the dock, passengers streamed out onto the walkway.

Finally, Eugenie, her cheeks pink from the chill, and looking all the prettier for it, emerged from the crowd and ontothe dock.

He strode toward her as other boat passengers streamed by. "Welcome to Canada, Eugenie." When he reached her, he leaned in and dared to brush his lips against her soft cheek.

With wide eyes, she looked up.. "Good to see you, Percy."

"I'm so delighted you could come." His broad smile almost hurt his face. He was so happy to see this strong, intelligent woman again. "My carriage is right over here."

He took her arm and led her there. Not nearly so fancy as his father's, in England, but very serviceable, nonetheless.

He called up to his driver, "Please take us to our venue." He assisted Eugenie inside his carriage.

Once settled, Percy rapped on the roof, for his driver to leave.

"Percy, I have a favor."

"What is it?"

"One of my mother's dear friends will be visiting from Mackinac Island."

"I've been there. It's beautiful."

"Yes. Well, she wishes to consult with an attorney, or in your case, a barrister, about a private matter. Someone who is the soul of discretion."

He leaned forward. "And you believe that would be me?"

"I do."

His chest warmed, despite the chill in the carriage. "Thank you for your confidence." He reached to grab the wool blanket on the opposite seat and spread it across Eugenie. Would there be many more such rides in which he would perform such an action? He fervently hoped so.

"I believe it's well deserved."

"When will this lady arrive?"

"That's part of the difficulty." She chewed her lower lip.

"Oh?"

"Christmastime."

"Ah." With his parents there, he'd have to make excuses.

"I know you're going to be terribly busy. But if you could give her even a short bit of your professional attention, I'd consider it a gift to me. A precious gift because Jacqueline brings my mother's memory to life for me. She means a great deal to me."

He patted Eugenie's gloved hand. "You've lost so much. Your mother. Your sweetheart. And now your father."

She sniffed and lowered her head.

"If there is someone who makes your burden lighter, I would do anything within my power to help—including coming over to Detroit to meet with her."

"Oh, Percy." She raised her head and locked gazes with him.

Should he kiss her? He longed to do so. He leaned forward and she didn't pull away. A sudden jolt, as they hit a rut, threw Eugenie into his arms.

She bumped her head into his chin. He bit back a groan of pain as he held her steady.

Eugenie laughed. "Are you all right? I fear I've injured your handsome face."

"You think me handsome?" He rubbed his sore chin. There might be a bruise later.

Again, she laughed. "I'm sure you know how attractive you are, Mister Gladstone."

He settled back in his seat but now he took her hand in his and held it. "I'd skate across frozen lake or river water to get to you and to help your mother's friend, if need be."

She drew in a deep breath. "That's why I can trust you. That's why. . ."

Why she loved him? Did she?

They rode on in companionable silence for the short remaining distance.

When they arrived, he assisted Eugenie from the carriage, longing to take her in his arms and kiss her right there. He wouldn't of course.

Percy called up to the driver. "Please return for us in two hours."

The man nodded in acknowledgement.

Standing before him, Eugenie, attired in a deep-charcoal wool cape with fur collar, looked stunning. She was far too beautiful and privileged for him. He glanced toward the cedar-sided building that resembled a massive cabin. Which might be what it was originally intended for—perhaps a building for trading furs. He exhaled slowly. What passed for a theater here in Windsor would be laughable on the American side, but it was all he had for entertainment.

Percy squared his shoulders and offered his arm to Eugenie. They followed a lumberjack dressed in ill-fitting clothing over the boardwalk and to the unvarnished pine entrance door. The big man held the door for them both, and Eugenie didn't bat an eyelash as they entered.

Lanterns hung overhead from the rafters and on the walls. At each end of the building, fireplaces provided limited heat. Seating was on long wooden benches strategically placed in the cavernous room, facing the makeshift stage.

Perhaps this had been a mistake inviting her here.

The theater building could have been one of Eugenie's father's hunting lodges, albeit without the antlers mounted on the walls. But it was warm. And Percy was with her, and that was what mattered. She'd not be a snob. But truly, fitted with this bustle, how would she manage two hours seated on a wooden plank?

"Let's find a seat." Percy pointed to the end of the back row, which was empty, and guided her along.

In the front row, a mother ineffectively tried to corral a half-dozen young children. In the second row, a matron grabbed the pipe that her husband was trying to light and pointed to a placard on the wall which forbid such a practice.

Movement from behind and a familiar voice distracted Eugenie. She turned to face the door. Horace entered with a pretty young woman on his arm.

Eugenie gasped. "What is Horace Ontevreden doing here?"

Percy narrowed his eyes. "That's him?"

"Yes. And is that your client?" Eugenie couldn't help cringing.

"That's not her and I don't know why he'd be here. But the show is open to the public, so I don't think I can do anything unless he bothers us."

"I don't think I can't stay here with Horace sitting over there." She recognized the woman he was with but couldn't place her.

If Eugenie was overdressed in her mourning clothes, then this young woman was even more out of place. Dressed in a deep-rose satin skirt with a contrasting white and navy plaid blouse, a blue short-waisted jacket, and a small cap affixed at an angle to her piled high red hair, the woman stood out like a lone cranberry fallen into a bowl of rice pudding.

"What would you like to do, Eugenie?"

And here she wasn't going to be a snob. She shook her head, not wanting to do anything that might cause trouble for Percy. He was, after all, a prominent member of this small community. "Can we please leave?"

"If you wish."

She felt dizzy and raised a hand to her brow.

Percy tucked her arm closer. "Let's go."

Horace and his lady friend hung their cloaks and Percy guided her out the door.

But where would he take her? "Oh my. Your driver left. I forgot."

He leaned in. "My home is but a block away. Can you walk it?"

She took in a fortifying breath. "Yes. Of course."

Percy grinned. "I can show you my home and that way you'll have a better idea of what to tell your ladies."

"A good idea. They may have a great many questions."

"My housekeeper can serve as chaperone if you wish." He quirked an eyebrow at her.

"Would she mind?"

"I don't believe so."

Outside, a gust of chill wind penetrated Eugenie's cloak, and she tugged the fur collar tighter around her neck. "Brr... I feel winter coming for certain."

Percy laughed. "And old Father Time isn't far behind Old Man Winter—with 1868 yet ahead of us in his capable hands. Well, not in Father Time's hands, but in the hands of God, who is Father of all."

He led her onto the roadway. A great deal of snow lay there except for in the wheel ruts. They stepped carefully forward.

Not far ahead of them, gas lights lit almost every room of an imposing three-story brick home. The rooms inside looked bright and cheery. "Who lives there, Percy, and why is it all lit up?"

"That's mine." He tapped the brim of his hat. "I despise coming home to a dark house, so the staff keeps the house well-lit until I return each night."

She widened her eyes. "I wasn't expecting so grand a home here."

She didn't have to say the unspoken—that he lived in a small backwater town in Ontario a fraction of the size of Detroit.

"I wanted a place where my..." He drew in a chill breath. "Where my family could come stay."

Straightening, Eugenie frowned. "But didn't you say this is the first time they've traveled to see you, and you've lived here—"

He raised his free hand. "Nigh on seven years now." With nary a visit from them.

"Oh." She frowned but didn't push the interrogation further.

He might as well push the margin. "I hope to fill all three stories with children someday, too."

"Oh!" Eugenie's suddenly cried out in pain and stumbled.

Percy caught her as she tripped over a fallen tree branch that was underfoot in the street. He held her elbows fast and looked down at her, her face in pain. "Are you all right?"

"Yes." She pulled free but took his hand as she stepped tentatively on one foot and then the other. "Ouch!"

A gentleman did what was needed. Percy scooped her up into his arms. "You're not taking another step on that foot until we have it looked at."

"What?" But she kept her arm wrapped around his neck. "You should put me down."

"I fear I may have caused part of the problem."

"How?"

"Forgive me for speaking of indelicate matters, Miss Mott." She fit perfectly in his arms.

Eugenie leaned her head on his shoulder. "So, you are not the committed bachelor that some believe you to be?"

"Certainly not." Three more strides and then he carried her up the four steps to the door. "Simply waiting for the right lady."

What would it be like to carry her into the house as his wife? He'd best put any such thoughts aside and be on his best behavior.

The front door opened, revealing his butler standing there, eyes wide. "Mr. Gladstone, what brings you back so soon? Is Miss Mott injured?"

"Yes, she's twisted her ankle."

Lemrich held the door for them and then closed it behind them.

"Please send Venus for the doctor."

"Yes, sir."

"I'll bring Miss Mott into the parlor, if you'll open that pocket door for me, please." Percy shifted her in his arms. He didn't want to drop his precious lady.

When Percy's servant had pushed back the door, the dear man carried her inside a cherry-paneled room. A rich burgundy, green, and gold wool carpet covered the floor. A fire burned in the hearth. Atop the mantel, tintype images, in silver frames, formed a long row. Percy set her on one of the rococo chairs.

"Is this a John Henry Belter chair?" Despite her pain, she couldn't help her interest. She ran her hand over the elaborate woodwork.

"Yes. My mother sent it with me from England."

"It's lovely." She winced as her foot began to throb.

"Let's put that foot up." He pulled a maroon ottoman closer and gently lifted her ankle. "I think I had better remove your shoe."

Eugenie frowned. "I have a bad feeling this is going to hurt."

"Likely so, but I'll be careful." His cheeks turned a shade of rose. "I'll have to lift your skirts up a little, too."

"It's all right."

A petite woman with skin the shade of strong tea strode into the room, hands on hips. "What's goin' on here, Master Percy?"

"Miss Mott has twisted her ankle, Sabina."

"I knows that, Lemrich done told me, but what you tryin' to do?"

"Get the boot off before her ankle swells further."

"Um, hum, I'm thinkin' I'll do that, Master Percy." She cast him a scolding look. "Now you shoo out of here."

"I'll be back in a moment, Eugenie." Percy departed.

"I'm Sabina—sort of cook and housekeeper rolled into one. But I'm thinkin' I'll be chaperone tonight."

Eugenie's cheeks heated. "I'm Eugenie Mott, from Detroit."

"I knows who you is, girl. You the gal got Master Percy's head on backwards the past month or two."

Eugenie laughed, but it made her foot hurt more and she groaned.

The tiny woman bent over her, gently undid her boot, then pulled it off little by little. "It's done swelled up bad."

Eugenie leaned forward to look and became lightheaded when she saw how large her ankle had become. "Oh my. I need to get home."

"You ain't goin' nowhere tonight, Missy Mott. Not on my watch." Sabina brushed her hands against her plaid apron. "Now let me have Master Percy get me some snow to pack on there."

Percy's servant departed, and Eugenie sat there, tears pooling in her eyes. She needed to get back to Detroit. She had to think of her ladies. And she had company coming to the area. She had to see Jacqueline and her family. They meant the world to her.

Soon Percy returned with a silver ice bucket. "Are you willing to try this possibly brutal treatment?"

She shrugged, her coat suddenly snug around her shoulders. She well knew how much it hurt to plunge one's foot into ice water. This, unfortunately, wasn't her first ankle injury.

Sabina joined them, a tray of what smelled like hot chocolate in her hands. She set it down on a nearby table. "Let's get you out of that coat, Miss Mott."

"But I must get home!" She struggled to cope with her pain and the situation she now faced.

"We'll see what the doctor says, Eugenie." Percy leaned close to her. "Let me and my staff take care of you."

What else could she do?

She would send a message to her household staff in the morning. And what about her Sugarplum Ladies? And the Swaines?

God, I trust Your plan. But does it have to be so painful?

Chapter Eight

C loves in your pickled tomatoes?" Eugenie leaned forward as Sabina used a fish fork to painstakingly remove the nubby cloves from the mason jar of tomatoes she'd just poured into a blue and white china bowl.

"They give it flavor, but you don't want to be eatin' a passel of whole cloves."

"My physician says they can be dangerous if you swallow them."

"That's why I'm removin' them, miss." Sabina's eyebrows tugged together as she bent over the bowl. She forked a dark clove out of the bowl and transferred it to a saucer. "There."

Eugenie inhaled the pungent aroma. "Are you sure you got them all?"

"Only put in twelve. And I got 'em all. So that's the trick— ya'll use my canned tomatoes, ya'll need to pull the dozen cloves out of each jar."

"All right." Eugenie shifted her foot on the wooden stool it was propped upon and picked up her menu cards.

"You got easy victuals planned for Christmas Eve and Christmas day." Sabina nodded in approval.

"And we have a subdued menu for the following five days." Eugenie tapped at her hastily written, recalled-from-memory receipts scattered on the large mahogany table that was beautifully inlaid with ebony. But how would she manage if her foot didn't heal?

"That make a week worth of 'em..." Sabina seemed to be leaving something unsaid.

Eugenie eyed the menus that she'd scribbled out earlier that morning. "Should we prepare a few back-up menus in case we can't find what we need?"

"Mr. Percy's folks'll be here soon. In a few days." Sabina frowned at the calendar. "Maybe ask your ladies to cook ahead a few things and bring 'em on over."

"That's a good idea." She should see what Mrs. Roat was putting together for Lorena and the Scott family. Eugenie moistened her lips. "My own cook will be enjoying the Southern fare that she and her sister ate in Virginia when they were growing up."

"My sister and I be doin' the same thing when I get to Ohio." Sabina grinned. "Just a few more days and then it'll be chitterlings, greens, corn pone, mm mm."

"I was thinking more of fried chicken, mashed potatoes, and gravy and biscuits."

"That goes without sayin'—that's Master Gladstone's favorite meal."

"Truly?"

"Truly."

"But won't his family want more traditional English fare?" At least they had a few more days to make quick adjustments.

Sabina went to the tall kitchen cabinet nearby and pulled out three stained cards. "His cook back home say his family love these." She handed them to Eugenie.

Eugenie scanned the paper. "Who doesn't love sugar cookies?"

Whistling, Percy strolled into the kitchen, hands tucked in his jacket pockets. "Sugar cookies?" He scanned the room.

"Not here!" Sabina placed her fists on her hips and cocked her head at him. "No, sir, not yet."

He puckered his lips in mock dismay. "And no Dutch apple pie?"

"A ham sandwich and tomato relish be enough for your lunch, Master Percy." Sabina clucked her tongue. "But them Sugarplum Ladies gonna spoil you while I'm gone."

Eugenie re-organized her receipts. "You said your mother eats like a bird, so I hope some good old American cooking might tempt her to eat."

"Father used to threaten Mother with a tray of seed to peck at if she kept eating like a bird."

"They got suet balls at the mercantile." Sabina quirked an eyebrow at her employer. "If'n you want Venus to run get you some before we go."

"I think not." Eugenie flinched as her foot spasmed.

In a flash, Percy's arms were around her and he lifted her from the chair. "Off you go. The doctor said this foot should be kept high and not on a low stool like that one."

Eugenie clung to Percy's neck as he carried her out from the kitchen, into the hallway, and up the stairs to the entryway. She felt breathless and she wasn't even the one doing the carrying.

"I'm going to put you to bed, right this instant." Percy's voice rang loud in the stairwell.

"Shhh, people will hear you!"

He carried her out to the hall as Lemrich opened the door. A half-dozen guests stood staring at them while a gust of icy breeze carried through the hallway. Eugenie felt Percy's shoulders stiffen and for a moment thought he'd lower her to stand, but he held her fast. "Welcome Mother and Father, Bard and wife! Or should I call you Lady and Lord Kent and Lady and Lord Cheatham? How lovely that you're early!"

Percy's parents and Eugenie gaped at one another.

Percy shifted her in his arms. "Let me get Eugenie situated, and I shall come back to greet you properly."

He carried her down the hall, and she couldn't help but be keenly aware of the gazes that followed them. The tall, distinguished-looking man had to be Percy's father and the stately woman his mother. The younger couple with them looked exhausted, with dark rings under their eyes. Had the older couple been so demanding? Or was it simply the long journey?

And she'd not realized that Bard and his wife, which Percy had called them, were also aristocrats with titles. Lady and Lord Cheatham. "Oh, Percy, I should go home."

"Nonsense, you heard what the doctor said. You're to stay put."

Soon he had her settled in the four-poster bed, her foot propped up on a feather pillow. A gentle rap sounded on the open door.

Mother hugged him and then moved gracefully to Eugenie's side and took her hand in hers. "I wondered when Percival would finally find himself a bride."

Eugenie's shocked expression almost made Percy chuckle.

Stepping beside him, Father coughed, covering a laugh, and then embraced Percy. When had he grown so thin? Percy could feel his father's ribs even beneath his thick tweed jacket. "My boy, it is so good to see you again."

"I'm so glad you could cross the pond, sir."

"Of course, I would. I'm just sorry it has taken so long."

Mother had settled down on the bed alongside Eugenie, as if they were long-separated friends. "You remind me of someone, my dear."

Father narrowed his eyes. "Indeed. Our Austrian friends' daughter."

"My mother was Austrian." Eugenie smiled up at Mother, but the pain lines around his beloved's eyes suggested she needed some rest.

Percy moved closer. "Do you need something for the pain?"

Eugenie dipped her chin.

Mother stood and he gave her another quick embrace. She wasn't one for much affection, but she returned a heartfelt squeeze.

Turning to face Eugenie, Mother cocked her head, her silver and chestnut curls bobbing against her pale cheeks. "We'll leave you to rest, my dear."

Percy emptied one of the medicinal powders into the glass on the bedside table and then poured water from the carafe into it. He stirred until it was dissolved. Then he assisted Eugenie to sit back up, placing an extra pillow behind her back. He handed her the glass.

She drank a few sips. "You go, be with your guests."

"My holiday staff arrived this morning while you were in the kitchen. I don't want you alone in here. I'll be sending one of them to sit with you for a while."

"Percy?"

"Yes?"

"Will you be telling your mother that we are not to be wed?"

He'd not become a barrister nor crossed an ocean by being faint of heart. "No. I doubt that will be necessary."

Percy waited for the "tell," the sign that he'd scored a point in the court of love. His heart thumped in his chest, and his breathing slowed as he waited. When Eugenie laughed, despite her pain, and a smile bloomed on her beautiful face, he had his answer. He exhaled the breath he'd been holding and bent and kissed her hand.

Now, to find a ring to go on her finger, to make her his.

That evening proved to be the best he'd ever spent with his family. His friend Bard and his wife took to their bed early and had only tea and toast before retiring. It had been a long journey.

The next morning as his parents and his friends slept late, Percy set to work. He'd carried Eugenie to the front parlor earlier. Now Percy paced the hall, checking how his new crew had done. Thank goodness Scipio hadn't wished to travel this Christmas and was helping organize the newcomers as the other servants prepared to depart. The paneling had been dusted and shone from the lemon oil that had been applied. The chandelier sparkled overhead. Even the brass door knocker glowed as they awaited the arrival of Eugenie's Sugarplum Ladies. The overflow of coats could be taken to the hall closet, which normally held Percy's black overcoat and umbrella and boots.

Why was he so anxious? Truth be told, he was more nervous about these ladies' opinions than that of his parents. He inhaled the scent of the holly garland and pine that one of the temporary workers had festooned from the stair rail.

A scene from long ago ran through his mind. The servants had all been lined up in the grand hallway to receive their Christmas boxes. Percy had hidden on the landing, behind the stair rails, looking down. He'd refused to accompany his family in the ceremony. He'd claimed he had a stomachache, but the truth was that he'd been embarrassed by the way his father condescended to the servants, who all year long worked so hard to make their life lovely—and Percy's own more bearable. His parents loved Percy, loved all of their children, and cared for their servants, but Mother and Father were a product of their own upbringing. He knew, even as a child, that he'd never as an adult live in such luxury. He'd had to look to their staff as he grew up to model for him what real work meant. Unlike his eldest brother, he'd have to earn his livelihood and he had.

He went to check on Eugenie. His sweetheart sat in the parlor sipping her tea while reading a treatise on *The Canadian Federation—The Dominion of Canada*. Strange how natural it seemed to have her there. Stranger yet was her choice of reading material.

"Should I try to find you something a little less esoteric?"

"My father discussed all of these changes with me last July, when they were occurring." She closed the narrow tome, but kept a finger at about the middle.

"I'm sure my own father would be glad to bore you with the details, too, if you'd allow him." He laughed.

Light shuffling announced his houseman. "Sir?"

"Yes?"

"The carriage has returned with the American ladies."

Percy stepped forward and parted the parlor's Irish lace curtains. "I don't see them."

From where she was seated, Eugenie turned and craned her neck to look.

When Percy turned back around, Scipio's eyes were downcast, color high on his dark cheeks. "They've come around to the back, sir."

"What?" Of course, that was how it was done, but these were Miss Mott's ladies—would she be offended?

Scipio clasped his hands at his waist. "Sabina asked if you'd like to greet them or if she should acquaint them with the kitchen first before she leaves."

Eugenie's shoulders slumped. "Oh, I wish they'd come see me first!"

Percy bent and squeezed her hand. "I'll go down and send them up to you, Eugenie."

Someone banged the brass knocker on the front door and Percy flinched. Scipio moved to open it and Percy followed him in the hallway to see who might be calling.

Rocking back and forth on his heels was a youth whose shaggy auburn hair, beneath his oversized wool cap, almost obscured his light eyes. He looked past the houseman at Percy.

"Got a message for ya, gov'nah." The boy's thick accent announced him as a recent British immigrant, likely from the East End. Was he one of the children who'd escaped to make his own way instead of being sent to a farm? The boy held out a grimy palm, his fingers and wrists covered with a makeshift moth-eaten mitten.

Percy plucked a coin from his vest pocket, stepped forward, and handed it to the urchin. "What is it?"

"Mrs. Jack-Will-Ine Swaine says send yer carriage to the station."

"Mrs. Jacqueline Swaine?" Eugenie's plaintive sigh carried into the hall. "Oh, my! I was supposed to see her in Detroit."

Percy had sent word to her staff that if they'd heard from Mrs. Swaine that she, and anyone with her, could be sent to his home. But he'd forgotten to tell Eugenie. "Mrs. Swaine has come here, then?"

"That's right, gov, her and a real pretty girl with her." The urchin scratched his cheek. "Sister of Lady Cheat-ham what's coming here, too, with her husband Lord Cheat-ham. Mrs. Swaine owns the Ca-dot ship what brought Miss Tumbles-town here."

"Ah yes, Lady Cheatham's sister was expected from Mackinac Island." Percy smiled at Eugenie.

"And Mother's dear friend, too? I wonder if Jacqueline brought Deanna down from the island with her on her husband's steamship."

"It looks that way." Percy leaned in. "I'm sorry but I'd forgotten to tell you, that I let Mrs. Swaine know you were here and she'd be welcome to visit with us in Ontario."

"Thank you." Her flushed cheeks revealed her excitement..

"Might not want to keep 'em waitin', guv." The child pushed a lock of greasy hair under his cap. Patting his pocket for another pair of matching coins, Percy retrieved them. "Here. Take this. Run to the station and tell them we're coming. I'll send my carriage."

A wide grin revealed the lad didn't yet suffer from tooth rot. "Will do."

Sudden conviction got ahold of Percy's tongue. "Come back here after and knock on the back door. I'll tell the staff to give you lunch with the new workers."

The boy touched his cap brim. "Much appreciated."

Percy might regret his offer later, but compassion reined now. "Where are you staying?"

The youth shrugged. "Here and there."

"If you need a place to lay your head, we've a hay loft over in the carriage house. And I could use a reliable errand boy."

"Yes, sir!" With a curt nod, the boy ran off.

Good heavens, unexpected guests were calling, his family was here after seven years, and his sweetheart had an injured foot. This was not the way he'd hoped Christmas would go. But he'd seen many a trial become complex and convoluted, and he trusted God would be at his side always.

How could he possibly complain, when he'd gone from a Christmas on his own to one full of loved ones? He couldn't.

Silver threaded through Jacqueline Swaine's dark hair now but she looked just as beautiful as ever. Eugenie accepted her mother's friend's embrace, and then gestured for her to sit in the nearby seat.

"Whatever did you do, dear?" Jacqueline pointed to Eugenie's foot. "We got the message from Mr. Gladstone that you were here and to stop by."

"I twisted my ankle the other night." She chewed her lower lip. "It might seem childish, but I was trying to get away from a man who'd been pursuing my hand in marriage. He's also tried to engage the attentions of another woman who'd actually sought Percy out."

"You don't say."

Kathleen wheeled in the tea cart. "I've got the Russian tea ready, if you'd like to be served."

Jacqueline sighed. "Oh my dear, I'd love some. It's been a long cold trip here."

With efficient movements, Kathleen poured the tea into a delicate gilded china cup and set it upon a matching saucer. "Sugar?"

"Two lumps would be lovely. Thank you." Jacqueline patted her coiled hair.

"I'll have the same, please." The pleasing scents of the spices and tea mingled in the air. "And Kathleen, could you please let the ladies know that my dear friend is here and I'll not be down until later."

"Yes, Miss Mott." Kathleen glanced between Jacqueline and her, a question in her eyes.

"Your mother was the dearest friend I ever had and I'm proud to call you my friend, too." Jacqueline smiled at Eugenie.

"I miss her so much." A tear trickled down her cheek.

"I, as well."

Kathleen handed the teacup and saucer to Jacqueline, who set it upon a nearby tea table.

"She loved her tea, didn't she?" Jacqueline reached for the teacup. "And I believe this Russian tea was one of her favorites.

"It was." Eugenie beamed up at Kathleen, who passed her the cup and saucer. "Thank you."

Kathleen dipped her chin and then rolled the cart from the room.

Jacqueline took a sip. "I remember once when we had Christmas at my hotel here. You, your mother, and father came. I had my husband, daughter, and my sons—God rest their souls—with me. It was a beautiful Christmas."

"Mother sent the servants off for a rest at Father's hunting lodge and they loved it."

Jacqueline laughed. "That place was something else, wasn't it?"

The two of them continued to exchange stories about Mother and Jacqueline's family for some time. It was as though this sweet woman brought with her a portion of Mother to share with Eugenie. Gratitude for this busy lady's presence renewed her spirit.

Jacqueline leaned in toward Eugenie. "I truly hate to bother Mr. Gladstone with my questions about how to protect my two remaining children. But when you wrote me that you trusted him totally, and then we received his message. . ."

"Of course, certainly he'll meet with you." Eugenie set her empty teacup down onto its saucer on the table.

"You'll bring him to the hotel so I can spend some more time with you and get to know him outside his legal capacity, too, right? Will you be able to stop and see the children?"

"I would love that. It's been too short a visit."

Someone rapped at the door. Kathleen stepped inside. "The ladies need some direction downstairs. They've all worked so hard, Miss Mott but we've had a situation come up with the courses for this evening."

"You must go help." Jacqueline stood. "May I assist you in walking?"

"No, but thank you." Eugenie stood and reached for her crutches, which had been found in the barn and cleaned off for her.

Percy strode into the room. "Mrs. Swaine, I'll be back in a moment to meet with you, but I have to carry this sack of lovely sugar down to the kitchen." He winked.

Jacqueline giggled like a schoolgirl and Eugenie's cheeks heated as he lifted her as though she indeed were a small sack of sugar.

Percy's arms were strong and he was careful to turn to avoid hitting her foot against any obstacles. "I imagine that Jaqueline's private questions about wills and codicils are best left to me."

"Indeed. And thank you, Percy."

"Any friend of yours is one to me."

"You're the best."

"Best barrister?" He scrunched up his face.

She laughed. "Just the best."

"All right then." He continued on down the stairs.

Eugenie patted his dark hair imagining what it would be like to have a little boy with similar locks. "I can only imagine how hard it must be to lose two children. She wants to make sure the other two are taken care of."

"I cannot fault her for wishing to ensure her estate is managed for the remaining two. But as a Canadian barrister, our laws are somewhat different from American. But I will advise her as best I can."

"I know she understands. We both appreciate you doing this, Percy."

"You're very welcome." He stopped his descent. "I'm glad I can help."

She leaned in and kissed his cheek. How she loved this kind man.

Soon, Percy had seated her by the second stove, and then departed upstairs.

Eugenie surveyed the groaning counters, piled high with all manner of food. She smiled at each lady in her crew. "You have all worked hard today."

Her Sugarplum Ladies had managed to become acquainted with the stoves and their peculiar functions and the ovens as well as where the bachelor kept his dishes, crystal, and silver stored. They'd prepared numerous side dishes as well as sauces and a pudding while ducks with apples roasted.

The *whack* of a branch against the nearby window made Eugenie flinch.

The ladies, except Tina, who was making cookies, and Adelaide who was acting as scullery maid, finished what they were working on and gathered around her. All sported pink cheeks from their efforts, but smiles, also.

Outside, the breeze escalated, casting dead leaves against the windowpanes. But the warmth in the kitchen and the sweet scent of cloves and cinnamon surrounded Eugenie. What if there was a storm when her crew needed to bring more catered goods to the house?

Don't borrow trouble.

Melissa, who'd become the leader of the group, clasped her hands at her waist. "This has been an excellent opportunity for us to practice catering private functions."

"Yes," Eugenie agreed. "And you had a difficulty you wished for me to address?"

Melissa and Deborah exchanged a long glance.

Deborah leaned in. "Lord Kent wishes to have both fish and game for this meal."

"And we have no wild game." Melissa shrugged.

Nearby, Nancy turned to stir a pot of lentil soup; the scent of celery, onions, and beef broth tickling Eugenie's senses.

"I think I saw duck in the icehouse—near the back." Eugenie was sure she had.

"There was only a small one." Deborah frowned.

"A number of you may go on to work on your own one day." And Eugenie would be so proud of them. "And you'll have to learn how to make do."

Kathleen nodded.

"What if we made a duck pâté and serve it with toast? Would that work?" Tina lifted a broken cookie to her lips and took a bite.

Melissa adjusted her apron. "Or mix mushrooms and rice with it to stretch it and serve on a small plate?"

"I'd say add it to a soup, but I've already got this one just about right." Nancy arched her eyebrows.

"All very good ideas." Eugenie pressed her hands together. "Pray tell me which one you think is best?"

"The pâté and serve it early." Kathleen crinkled her nose. "That way he can't complain."

"Or serve it later after he's had all those wines that he's requested served with the meal," Nancy said.

When the women broke into laughter, Eugenie waved her hands crosswise to stop them. "That's enough now. I think the Brits are used to doing things differently over there."

"Duck pâté it is, then." Melissa smiled.

That woman was a born leader. It may be time to bring her on as staff for their training center.

Pausing from cutting out Percy's requested sugar cookies, Tina looked up from the table. "Thank you for bringing us here and for having us prepare some of Mr. Gladstone's favorite recipes today. I've really enjoyed it."

By the window, Adelaide stopped peeling potatoes. "I couldn't say one bad thing about this place."

"Nor I," echoed the others.

"I believe his staff feels the same way." Eugenie was sure of it.

Sleet tapped at the row of kitchen windows, the gray skies outside promising a storm. Eugenie frowned. "We should pray for Sabina, Lemrich, and Venus in their travels."

As the wind gusted, wet sleet and ice rattled the panes against the window frame. In the corner, the young messenger boy finished stuffing a roll into his mouth. He looked outside and shivered.

"We'll make a pallet on the floor for you to sleep on." Eugenie pointed to a warm corner of the room.

"No, miss. Master Gladstone said I could sleep in the barn loft."

Deborah shook a wooden spoon at him. "Not tonight you won't."

Kathleen quickly scooped a small amount from each of their dishes onto a dinner plate. "Come sit down and sample our meal for the night."

Eyes wide as saucers, the boy shook his shaggy head.

Melissa laughed softly. "The Sugarplum Ladies request your presence at our table." She patted the seat beside her.

Eugenie blinked back tears as the boy slowly rose and went to sit at the table. This was what Christmas was truly all about.

Loving others as Christ would love us.

Adelaide cast a shy glance at the boy, who wasn't much younger than her. Her mother's note had indicated that the girl could stay as long as was necessary. The way the note was written, it didn't sound as though the separation would cause the woman much distress. Perhaps it was because she was so ill. That had to be it.

Deanna Tumbleston entered the kitchen, her curls bobbing around her pretty face. "Lord Percival has finished chatting with Mrs. Swaine."

Lord Percival indeed. Eugenie almost snorted. But it was true. He could rightfully claim that title. If he wished. Which obviously he didn't. She smiled, her esteem for him rising even further. And how good of him to take time to advise her mother's friend.

"And she bids you to come say your good-byes, as she wishes to depart for the last ferry before the storm comes in." Deanna came forward and squeezed Eugenie's arm. "Mrs. Swaine has been a good friend to me on the island, despite the difference in our ages. I know she loves you very much and misses your mother dearly."

"Yes. I feel the same." Tears pricked her eyes as Eugenie gave the younger woman a quick hug. "Let me bid her adieu."

Oh Lord, bring all travelers safely to their destinations. In Jesus's precious name, Amen.

Chapter Nine

*A*ttired in formal dinner wear, Percy tugged at his cravat as he strode down the hall in his snug-fitting gray and black plaid wool flannel trousers. Caroline stood in the hallway outside Eugenie's room, tapping her toe. "Hurry up, Barden."

"Coming." Bard emerged from Eugenie's room, carrying Percy's wide-eyed darling.

Despite his friend being a married man, jealousy coursed through Percy. "What are you doing carrying Eugenie?"

Deanna waved him back. "We're trying to get her to the table and seated."

Eugenie's cheeks reddened and she ducked her head against Bard's pristine white collar, sending another surge of jealousy though Percy.

Barden lumbered like a woodsman carrying a load of logs. "Out of my way, old man!"

"Don't drop her!" Percy snapped, then instantly regretted it as he looked up to the stairway to see his mother's stern look of disapproval.

Father took Mother's arm and led her down.

Where was the temporary butler? Percy waved everyone on. "Let's move to the dining room."

Deanna slid into her chair. "These are so much more comfortable than those ship benches that were bolted down to the floor."

Barden installed Eugenie in her seat next to Percy as the rest of the guests took their places.

The hall clock chimed the hour and the first of the servants appeared. She dipped a curtsy. "Soda water is prepared, sir."

Father sent the girl a scathing look. "Lady Kent and I shall have claret with the meat course and white wine with the fish."

Eugenie cleared her throat. "There is no fish course."

Percy laid a gentle hand on her shoulder as he addressed his father. "Not tonight, sir." But he'd go over the next night's menu and feed Father a sardine if that's what it took to satisfy his demand for a fish course. Where did he think he was? This was not some grand estate with a permanent full kitchen staff.

"We have a lovely trout almondine for tomorrow." Eugenie took a sip of soda water.

"Good." Was that Percy's imagination or did Father look a little embarrassed at his outburst? He kept his eyes averted as another servant filled his crystal goblet half-full with claret.

The servants continued to fill the goblets with soda water, wine, or apple cider.

"Shall we toast the queen?"

Mother raised her goblet. "To Victoria."

Hard to believe Mother's childhood friend was now queen of England.

After they'd made their toasts, the Americans somewhat awkwardly, Percy rose. "I shall lead us in prayer."

Perhaps it was the flickering gaslights that caused the sheen he saw in Mother's and Father's eyes before both bowed their heads.

Eugenie tried to keep her head down, waiting for Percy's mother's first volley of criticism. When would the bombardment begin? Hadn't her sweetheart said she was very peculiar about what she ate? Seated beside Percy, attired in his finest, Eugenie regretted her dark mourning clothes. But she was keenly feeling the loss of her father. Across from them, Percy's father coughed. He had the look her own father had, before...

Pray dear God, not Percy's father, too.

Lady Caroline was the only one at the table with an appetite, it seemed. The servers had given her seconds on everything.

Pausing between bites, the pretty woman beamed at Percy. "This is a beautiful home, Mr. Gladstone."

"Thank you. And please, call me Percy."

"And a lovely meal, Eugenie."

Eugenie flushed with pleasure. "Thank you, Lady Caroline."

The American woman waved her hand in protest. "No need to call me that. It feels quite odd. Just plain old Caroline is fine."

Barden's eyebrows drew together. "It's been a very strange journey for us. I don't wish to cast a pall over dinner by discussing it, though."

Percy cast a sideways glance at Eugenie as he took a bite of the duck. He'd told her earlier that Barden had lost his father, his two brothers, and an infant nephew in a short time. He'd also had to return to England recently to live, even though he'd made a new home in Kansas with his wife. So many changes.

Pretty dark-haired Deanna gave her brother-in-law a saucy wink. "Barden's title doesn't give me much more respect at the fort—because most of the soldiers met Barden when he was washing up dishes and tossing slops at our inn back in Kansas."

Percy's parents' eyebrows rose at exactly the same moment and Eugenie stifled the urge to laugh. Lady Kent set her fork down and placed her hands in her lap. *Oh dear, there are several more courses to be served yet.*

"Can you recommend any entertainments on the American side?" Lord Kent aimed his query at Eugenie.

She named the many festivities they could attend. Each guest expressed a desire in a different outing. This could get hectic traveling back and forth. And Eugenie was in no shape to join them. "Of course, you can only engage in these pursuits if weather permits."

Percy gestured to the servants to remove the first set of dishes. "Remember, we'll have several beautiful church services to attend. Although the Anglican church is small, they boast a lovely choir. Granted, most of the singers are either lumberjacks, natives from the area, or newer residents who escaped from the South on the Underground Railroad."

Eugenie anticipated his parents' shocked expressions, but they were not forthcoming.

"Of course, dear." His mother waved a hand airily at him. "That goes without saying."

As the next course was served, Eugenie held her breath. She could picture her Sugarplum Ladies downstairs, awaiting the verdict on their creations. So far, everything had been sublime.

Conversation turned briefly to politics, music, theater, and a heated debate as to whether Dickens or Thackeray was the more literary writer. Much laughter and a few taunts between Barden and Percy as well as Percy and his father had Eugenie's sides in a stitch. By the time dessert was served, she knew the evening had been a success.

Lord Kent pushed away from the table. "I've not indulged in such fine fare in a long time."

Percy leaned in. "Well done, my dear."

Patting his lean midsection, Barden made a face of consternation. "If we keep this up, we'll be fatter than the stuffed goose by Twelfth Night."

Twelfth Night? Eugenie suddenly recollected that the British followed a different tradition than most Americans. Maybe it was related to Church of England or Anglican traditions. She quickly searched her memory as to when Twelfth Night began. She bit down on a sugar cookie and chewed as she considered.

"Will you be staying though Epiphany, then?" Caroline smiled warmly at Eugenie.

That was it. *Christmastide extends into January.* She couldn't swallow. She began to choke on her cookie.

Percy patted her back. "Are you all right?"

Eugenie shook her head, covering her mouth with her napkin, coughing.

"Here, take a drink." Percy pushed her goblet toward her.

Eugenie sipped the soda water until the spell passed.

All eyes seemed fixed upon her.

Her church did not celebrate Epiphany. "Uh, that's January fourth? Or fifth?"

"Epiphany is the sixth of January." Lady Kent cast a glance between Eugenie and Percy.

Her ladies had gotten the dinner just right. Too bad Eugenie hadn't done the same for her ladies' contract.

Now what was she to do?

It was Christmas eve morning and most of the guests had occupied themselves in the parlor. Her Sugarplum Ladies needed to know of her error. Eugenie had spent the morning having a fascinating discussion with Lord Kent. He was keenly interested in business. Since Eugenie had grown up discussing such things with her father, she'd enjoyed sharing her thoughts with him. And the man genuinely seemed appreciative. She still sorely missed her father, but Lord Kent's presence had brought her some comfort.

Percy emerged from his study. "Eugenie, how is your foot this morning?"

"Improved, but still sore." It was several shades of purple. "But I need to go down to the kitchen and speak to the ladies."

"Certainly." He bent toward her.

She wrapped her arms around Percy's neck as he lifted her from the settee, her heartbeat kicking up a notch. The curls around his collar tickled her hands and she relished his warm breath against her cheek.

"I'll carry you downstairs just this once, and then you must allow your Sugarplum Ladies to work their magic." Although his voice was stern, she could feel his chest constricting as though he was holding back laughter.

"On my honor, sir, I shall endeavor to remain upstairs thereafter." *Today at least.*

Lord Cheatham laughed. "That's a good girl."

Caroline took her sister's arm and pulled her up from the wing-back chair at the fire, where she was knitting a red and navy scarf. "Come on. Let's take a look outside."

"Oh no," Eugenie protested. "Please, Lady Caroline, rest." She'd learned Caroline was expecting her first child.

"She has no intention of resting. If you don't take her to the kitchen, I shall be forced to skate upon yon pond with her." Lord Cheatham pointed toward the wavy frosted windowpanes. Across the field, a pond had already frozen over.

Deanna wagged a finger at her brother-in-law. "You'll be skating over there within the hour, so get your warm clothes on, Bard."

One of the servants carried in another armful of wood for the fire as Percy carried Eugenie out into the hall. She could get used to the wonderful feeling of having him so close.

"Your mother and I are going for a jaunt in the sleigh." Father crooked his finger for the servant to come over. "Fetch us our coats, boots, and hats, and have the carriage man hook up my boy's sleigh, would you?"

"Yes, sir."

Percy feigned a scowl at his father as he stopped by the stairs to the kitchen. "I see you feel quite at home here, Father."

"Keep those Sugarplum Ladies feeding him and I shan't be able to get him to return home, dear." Lady Kent rose up on tiptoes to kiss Percy's cheek.

Oh my. When should Eugenie tell Percy that her workers would be leaving in several days?

Something was awry with Eugenie besides her aching foot. But Percy knew better, as a barrister, when to push for information and when to wait. For now, he'd be patient.

He returned from downstairs to find several of his servants shoving a pine tree through his front door. "What's this?"

"Lord and Lady Kent requested it."

"In honor of the queen."

Barden looked up from sharpening his borrowed skates. "Queen Victoria does love her Christmas trees."

Outside, snow floated around his mother and father as they waved from the sleigh heading down his drive. Percy's household had completely gone out of his control.

He'd arranged for an extra rented carriage to be sent from the livery for their travel to church that evening. The Christmas "crackers" had been delivered with the one specified for Eugenie left empty for him to fill.

Earlier, Mother had gifted him with Grandmother's diamond

ring, which she'd brought with her. "I read something between the lines on your missives, Percy," she'd told him. "I saw Eugenie may be the one for you—of which your father and I heartily approve." Percy patted his pocket, feeling the ring there, and grinned.

A servant carried in the newspaper and presented it to Percy. "Thank you."

He sat in the parlor as the others began setting up the tree. When they placed it directly in front of the window, blocking his light, he stood, retaking his ground in his own home. "Bring that to the dining room."

Soon they were gone, leaving the scent of pine, as well as a trail of needles. Percy sighed and opened the Detroit newspaper. Nothing much on the front page. But when he reached the social page, he stilled. Beside a picture of the happy couple was the headline: Horace Ontevreden to Wed Canadian Heiress. His jaw dropped.

"What's wrong?" Bard stood in the parlor entryway, dressed for a blizzard.

Percy shook his head and scanned the article before he began to laugh as he recognized the pseudonym that Miss Menter, the titian-haired street walker, had used. Would such a union be valid? And what would Mr. Ontevreden do when he learned the truth of his betrothed? Sometimes there was justice in the world.

The man had been taken in by someone even more scheming than himself.

The Christmas Eve service and the dinner couldn't have gone any better. But only two of Eugenie's helpers could stay past Monday, the day before New Year's Eve.

Deanna, Caroline and Barden sat with Eugenie and made easy meal plans.

"I can't believe you're willing to help with the other work, too." Eugenie gestured around the dining room. "We had those two young women from town who'll come in, but there will still be much work."

Barden waved his hand. "This particular Lord is well acquainted with cleaning, cooking, and the like."

"If it wasn't for the Tumbleston Inn needing help, I'd never have met Bard." Caroline rose up on tiptoe and kissed her husband's cheek.

"We'll still have two of my ladies, I'll be here, and with your help and the girls from town we should be fine." Eugenie exhaled a breath of relief. Never again would she forget Epiphany and how the Anglicans celebrated Christmas. "Oh, and little Harry, the new errand boy, can surely assist us."

The others nodded in agreement. What a different Christmas this had been from what she'd planned. God was bringing her the blessings of friends and family not only to herself but to her servants and to these ladies under her care. She loved her work and her Sugarplum Ladies—but she could also see that they were getting ready to fly out on their own in some capacity in their upcoming events. They would be leaving the nest, so to speak. And God had brought a wonderful, intelligent, and caring man into her life at a time when she was sure she'd remain unmarried. Could she even possibly hope that one day she would indeed be a mother? Perhaps to many children? Was it not too late?

What would 1868 hold? Would she be in this house again, celebrating Christmastide with Percy?

"I'm going to find Percy." He'd asked her to meet him in the parlor when the four of them were finished talking.

Using her crutches, she took her time and maneuvered down the hallway. Upstairs, soft conversations continued behind closed doors.

A maid moved past her, head down. "Excuse me, milady."

Everyone in the house had become "milady" in the past few days. She'd even heard one of the servants whisper that there might be a new "Lady" in the house soon.

Eugenie paused, clutching her crutches, then took a tentative step. Her ankle was less swollen and discolored, and only a little painful. The crutches were a blasted nuisance.

Footfalls carried from the parlor and Percy stood there, hands on hips. Was he so terribly angry with her? He certainly could have been clearer in telling her what he'd wanted with her.

"Can you manage?"

"I think if I walk slowly, I'll be better off than with these things." She leaned the crutches against the wall.

Thankfully, both feet felt steady beneath her. She smiled tentatively until she caught Percy's sharp gaze. Was he considering how she was out of his parents' and friends' aristocratic set? The daughter of a businessman. Some businesswoman she was—failing to learn the end date of an agreement.

He held his arm out for her. It was time to go home. But who would help Percy when the ladies left?

The parlor was fully lit and the cherrywood card table had been opened, with two chairs seated adjacent one another. An inkstand and pen stood at the ready, with a sheet of creamy paper laid out that had a list numbered one through seven with brief notations made afterward. What was going on?

Percy pulled out a shield-backed chair and helped her sit. She adjusted her skirts around her. "You look like you're about to write a legal brief."

"I am." A smile tugged at his perfect lips. "A contract, since we've gotten this agreement with your Sugarplum Ladies mixed up."

"I'm sorry, Percy—"

He raised his hand as he took his place and dipped the pen into the well.

Eugenie shook her head. "This is truly beyond the pale, to think you would draw up a contract now."

"Eugenie—"

She interrupted him this time. "No. I will not have my ladies losing out on anything you have promised them, not even if I have to stay and perform the duties myself."

Someone hiccupped nearby. "Good idea!" Lord Kent rose, hoisting an empty brandy carafe.

"Father!" Percy rose but his father gestured for him to sit. "I didn't realize you were lurking there."

"If you don't marry her, you're a fool." He set the crystal container down and stumbled from the room, humming, "On Christmas Day in the Morning."

The color seemed to have drained from Percy's face. "Well, I guess you've discovered Father's little secret hobby, too."

Eugenie bit her lip. It wasn't for her to judge.

"At least Father isn't dying, which is what I feared." He quirked an eyebrow at her.

"So his 'illness' is a little more complicated than you thought."

"Quite so." Percy gestured toward the document. "And this has nothing to do with household cooking. Caroline, Deanna, and even Barden have volunteered to help."

"Yes, they just told me. I'm so relieved."

"The Tumblestons and Bard did, after all, run an inn in Kansas."

"Yes, I know you'd mentioned that was how your friend had met his wife."

Percy rubbed his chin. "I still can't believe Caroline had Barden cleaning up slops and the like. Egad."

"But what is your brief about? Do I need to witness something for Jacqueline?"

"No. But I welcome you to review this proposal."

She leaned forward and read the writing scrawled across the top.

Wherein our petitioner's heart has been stolen by Eugenie Mott of Detroit, Michigan, it is deemed only proper and fitting that Miss Mott shall:

1) Surrender her heart in return,

2) Promise herself evermore to be known as the wife of the petitioner, Percival Gladstone.

She stopped reading as tears blurred her vision.

Percy dropped down on one knee and took her hand in his. "If you'll agree to my terms, then you shall make the petitioner the happiest barrister in all of the Dominion."

"I will."

Percy slid the ring onto her finger then leaned in. He kissed her so thoroughly that dizziness threatened to overcome her. Thank goodness she was seated else she might have swooned.

Someone clapped in the hallway and then there was a distinct hiccup. As they broke the kiss, Lady and Lord Kent peeked in.

"Does Grandmother's ring fit, darling?"

"Perfectly." Percy raised Eugenie's arm up, the diamond flashing back light from the lamps.

"Wasn't going to ask this now…" Percy's father exchanged a telling look with his wife. "But might a wedding take place before we return home?"

"Yes." Eugenie and Percy's voices joined in agreement.

"You've just given us the best Christmas present." Percy's mother wiped tears from her eyes. "That of seeing our son happy, loved, and living a godly life."

Percy's father nodded in approval. "What every parent wishes for."

Surely that was what her father had wanted for Eugenie when he'd tried to marry her off to Horace. But God's ways really weren't man's ways.

Eugenie would never have envisioned the future that was before her now. But God had known all along.

And she could trust His plans.

The End

Author's Notes

This is a fictional story. While there was a Marquessate of Kent, by the time of this story, 1867, there was no Marquess of Kent, as I've titled Percy's father. Similarly, fictional Barden Granville IV didn't inherit any real-life Earldom of Cheatham Hall—which is named for a military base near where I live. On a personal note, my great-grandparents were from Maidstone, in the UK, which is why I chose that location. Also, my father loved taking us to some gardens in Windsor, Ontario, so I placed Percy there awaiting his Victorian Christmas.

The Historical Society of Michigan's magazine included a story about Detroit socialites who assisted Civil War widows in learning to make a living by catering. That article inspired this story. While I "borrowed" the Mott name, I have no indication that the Mott family was involved in this venture. Eugenie was named for and inspired by the beautiful Austrian princess Eugenie. I also had a great-aunt by the name of Eugenia.

The Detroit and Windsor areas did have a huge influx of both escaped slaves on the Underground Railroad and post-Civil War freed African-Americans. Unfortunately, many people had been separated from their family members, some to parts unknown. So both households in my story have African-American servants being reunited with family members.

Many of the unusual recipes or food preparation activities are from Worbly's Magazine of 1867. Thank you to the writers who have revived the Worbly's Magazine for modern readers.

Wool flannel is a thing. It's not like we think of as flannel. Wool flannel is cloth with a nice drape and is used for making clothing such as the trousers that Percy wore.

The expression that someone has "got your number" which I used in this story, originated in the mid-1800s, and was used by Charles Dickens in one of his books. We associate the expression with telephone number usage, but such is not the origin of usage.

The Morris chair, which reclined, was indeed introduced during the time frame of this story. How I enjoy our own recliners at home! I like to think Eugenie well appreciated hers, too.

Readers will recognize many characters from my other stories who make appearances here in this novella—some from *My Heart Belongs on Mackinac Island: Maude's Mooring*, such as Jacqueline Cadotte Swaine. Some (Sisters Caroline and Deanna Tumbleston and Barden AKA Lord Cheatham) are from my novella, "Dime Novel Suitor" (which will release as a standalone novella at a later date) from *Seven Brides for Seven Mail-Order Husbands*. The Scott family characters come from my debut in Christian fiction *Return to Shirley Plantation*. I was so delighted to reunite Angelina with her half-sister, Lorena, who works for our heroine Eugenie in this story.

A number of characters from this story appear in my novella, "*Love's Beacon*," which originally appeared in Barbour's *The Great Lakes Lighthouse Brides Collection*. You may wish to read *Love's Beacon* next—but I won't give a spoiler as to why! Love's Beacon will be expanded and developed into a full-length novel for release in 2024.

Acknowledgements

Thank you, God, that you allow this cracked vessel to journey on and to write stories for Your glory. Thank you to my family members, who support my writing. I am extremely blessed to have my wonderful critique partner, Kathleen Maher, an amazing author and editor. God bless my editor, Ellen Tarver, for her hard work on the original version of the novella. Many blessings to Stacey Ulferts who stepped into the breach and sent me line edits on this new version of The Sugarplum Ladies. Any errors are my own.

King's College Cambridge, 2008, Victorian-era carols on YouTube were the inspiration music for my story. Simply beautiful. Thank you to the friends who allowed me to borrow their names for this story—Carrie Booth Schmidt's and Carrie Moore Gould's names came together for fictional Carrie Booth Moore's name (a character who also appears in my novella "Love's Beacon" originally published in *The Great Lakes Lighthouse Romance Collection*). I also borrowed names from my best friend, Tara Mulcahey, and my son's friend, Christian Zumbrun, and many more!

Thank you to the members of the Avid Christian Fiction Readers group on Facebook for their feedback. My Pagels' Pals members have been a great support—thank you all! Thank you to early reader/reviewers, too: Sherry Moe, Tina Rice, and Joy Ellis!

A Recipe for Sugarplums

Traditional sugarplums are made with dried fruit and other things. The common fruit is often prunes. Yup—prunes. My mother made a variant of traditional sugarplums, made with date. I think if sugarplums had been called prune balls (prunes are made from certain types of plums) then a lot of people probably would not have eaten them!

My mother coated her confection with coconut and occasionally with slivered or crushed almonds, as more traditional recipes sometimes do. Occasionally it was with decorative large crystal sugar.

We love dried apricots at my house, so a recipe with these in the mix plus walnuts is more appealing to my family.

Start with fresh soft dates using ten to twelve large ones. Medjool dates work well. You can either use your food processer on them or do the old-fashioned way of smashing them up with a fork. If your dried fruit is somewhat hard, then it would help to moisten them with some water and bring them to a boil on the stove to soften them. My mom used to do that with the dried dates she used, which looked like little pellets!

You can also add in chopped nuts or oats if you wish, with the dried fruit, but don't overdo it.

Form the smashed/processed prunes/dates or dried fruit into balls and place on waxed paper on tray in fridge.

Thirty minutes later, roll the fruit balls in flaked coconut or sugar or crushed nuts like almonds. Return to the fridge.

Sanding Sugar, or decorative sugar with large crystals, can be used to decorate the sugarplums and you can also dye the sugar crystals to make colorful sugarplums. You have to let the dyed sugar dry before you roll the balls in it.

Store the sugarplums in a tightly sealed container. Enjoy!

Bio:

Carrie Fancett Pagels, Ph.D., is the award-winning and bestselling author of over twenty Christian fiction books. Twenty-five years as a psychologist didn't "cure" her overactive imagination! A self-professed "history geek," she resides with her family in the Historic Triangle of Virginia but grew up as a "Yooper" in Michigan's beautiful Upper Peninsula.

Connect with me at: www.carriefancettpagels.com

While you're browsing my website, be sure to sign up for my newsletter via the Contact page. You can also send me messages via the Contact page form. You can see some of my other books on my website Books page.

You can also find me on Facebook, Instagram, Pinterest, Twitter, and YouTube (where I share some videos of me reading sections of some of my stories!

If you enjoyed this novella,

a review is always appreciated!

Made in the USA
Middletown, DE
04 November 2022

14021012R00056